MW00978904

Don't Bug Me!

Don't Bug Me!

PAM ZOLLMAN

Holiday House / New York

Library of Congress Cataloging-in-Publication Data
Zollman, Pam.
Don't bug me! / by Pam Zollman.—1st ed.
p.   cm.
Summary: When Megan must collect twenty-five insects for a school project, her
little brother's interference and a classmate's teasing make the task difficult, and
reveal that she does not know either of them as well as she thought.
ISBN 0-8234-1584-8
[1. Insects—Fiction.   2. Brothers and sisters—Fiction.   3. Teasing—Fiction.
4. Schools—Fiction.   5. Friendship—Fiction.]   I. Title.
PZ7.Z76 Do 2001
[Fic]—dc21
00-048225

Dedicated to
my husband, Bill,
and my two sons, Keith and Bryan,
for their loving patience,
encouragement,
and support.

Special thanks to
Marilyn Evans, Sydnie Kleinhenz, Ginny Roeder, Kathy Duval,
Ila Rae White, Peggy Shallock, and Mary Jane Hopkins
for helping me hatch this book.

Special thanks to
Serena Chea, Layne Johnson, Betty Traylor Gyenes,
Melanie Chrismer, and Kelly Bennett
for helping me nurture and feed my book.

Special thanks to
Regina Griffin and Michelle Frey
for giving wings to my book
and showing it how to fly.

Don't Bug Me!

chapter
1

Screams from the girls' bathroom echoed down the hall. I'd been on my way back to class after lunch, but those screams made me rush back the way I'd come.

Only two things make us girls scream like that.

Boys—or bugs!

Just as I reached the bathroom door, Charlie Bettencourt bumped into me. The prime suspect at the scene of the screams, Charlie could never hide his guilt. If it weren't for his cute smile, he wouldn't get away with anything.

"What'd you do now?" I asked.

Charlie tried to look innocent. "Me? Why nothing, Megan." He grinned, showing his dimples. "Except maybe dare Oscar to kiss Rita."

"He wouldn't!"

More shrieks made us both turn back toward the door.

Shrugging, Charlie said, "Sounds like maybe he did."

I shouldered my way through everyone inside and found my best friend, Belinda. "What happened?" I asked. "Did Oscar kiss Rita?"

"Even better," she told me, her face flushed with excitement. "A roach!" She spread her arms wide. "Megan, it's the biggest, hairiest tree roach I've ever seen."

I tried to peer through the crowd. A swarm of girls huddled in one corner, trapping the insect between them and the sinks. "Roaches aren't really hairy, are they?" I asked.

Belinda shrugged. "Ask Tamika. It flew right in her face."

"Oh, gross!" I said, wrinkling my nose.

I could see the back of Tamika's head, her dark, tight curls bobbing. She had her sneaker in one hand, and she was trying to herd the reluctant roach into it. Last year she would have squished that bug flat. This year she acted like a concerned cowboy trying to round up a beloved stray.

Since our school, DeMitri Intermediate, is only for sixth graders, we all have the same science assignments. And our current assignment is to capture and kill twenty-five different insects, pin them to corkboard, and label them.

Most of us girls would have run away from a bug last year in elementary school. Not this year. Now we all run toward a bug, hoping to catch it. Insects don't have a chance in our school. Personally I think it's a plot to save on the cost of exterminating the building.

Now, I don't like bugs any better than last year. They're nasty, and I shudder when I have to pick one up. But those bugs will help me pass science. And, believe me, I need all the help I can get.

Shrieking again, the crowd parted when the roach tried to escape. As it scurried toward me, I saw it clearly.

It was huge! A true monster!

Before it reached me, Tamika scooped it up in her shoe, covered the opening with her hand, and yelled in triumph.

"Hey," Charlie Bettencourt called from the bathroom doorway, "what's all the shouting about?"

"Bugs," Belinda said. "Tamika found a huge one."

He looked disappointed. "So it wasn't about Rita?"

"I'm going to warn her," I said.

Charlie grinned, his dimples showing in full force. "That wouldn't be any fun, Megan. Here comes Mrs. Matzke." He hurried down the hall in the opposite direction.

Two seconds later our history teacher stood in the doorway, hands on hips, frown on face. "What's going on in here?" she demanded.

"Tamika caught a roach," Belinda explained. Some of the girls behind me grumbled in disappointment.

"All right, everyone clear out of here," Mrs. Matzke said. "Get back to your classes."

As we filed out, the teacher put a firm hand on Tamika's shoulder. "You and I are going to find a container for that roach."

Grinning, Tamika held up her sneaker. "It's a beaut, Mrs. M. Want to see it?"

"Most certainly not!" The teacher prodded Tamika toward the science room, keeping a wary eye on the sneaker in Tamika's hand. "Be sure that thing doesn't get out."

Belinda whispered, "I wish it would. Then maybe I could catch it."

"I know where you can get lots of insects," I said. "But they won't let us go there."

"Where?"

I giggled. "The school kitchen."

Belinda pretended to gag. "I just ate lunch! Thanks a lot, Megan."

"What are friends for?"

Belinda looked behind her, then on both sides, checking if anyone could hear her. "Maybe we *should* raid the kitchen sometime," she whispered.

"You're crazy!" I laughed. "You don't really mean it . . . do you?"

"You're right. It's a crazy idea."

Charlie Bettencourt was standing near the door to our English class. "What's crazy?"

"You," said Belinda, "for daring Oscar to kiss Rita."

He shrugged. "He said he liked her."

"That was an awful dare. Poor Rita!" I said.

Charlie followed me into the classroom. "It doesn't matter. Oscar would never do it, anyway."

"But you embarrassed him," I scolded.

Dimples creased Charlie's cheeks. "Yeah, his face did turn a nice shade of red. So, what embarrasses you, Megan?"

I didn't reply. Instead, I flopped down in my seat. My cheeks suddenly flushed, and I didn't know why.

Miss Rosenbloom began teaching us the merits of diagramming sentences. I couldn't see any merits in that. Nor could I see any merits in Charlie Bettencourt. He was as much of a pest as my little brother.

When school was finally over, Belinda and I sat next to each other on the bus, as usual. Tamika sat across the aisle, showing everyone her monster roach in a glass jar.

The moment Oscar stepped through the bus doors, Charlie led the boys in making smacking, kissing noises. Before Oscar ducked his head, I saw his face flame with color. Even his ears and the back of his neck were burning. I was glad Rita didn't ride the same bus.

Belinda leaned close to me and whispered, "I heard Charlie likes you."

"Me?" My mouth dropped open. "Well, I can't stand him."

"You talk to him all the time."

"So do you."

Belinda smiled. "But it's not me he likes."

"I don't believe it," I said indignantly.

She shifted her backpack to the floor and put her feet on top. "He said the only reason he doesn't sit next to you on the bus is because of our assigned seats."

"Did he tell you this?"

"No, Hector did."

I frowned. Hector Salinas and Charlie had been best friends since fourth grade when Charlie moved here. Was Belinda right?

"Hey, Megan," Tamika called, "how many bugs do you have?"

"Not as many as you do," I said. "How about giving me your roach?"

She clutched the jar close to her heart. "No way. I worked hard to capture Bob."

Belinda laughed. "You named it?"

"I name all my bugs," Tamika said.

"So how are you going to kill it?" I asked.

"In the freezer," she said. "I just can't do it any other way."

"Me neither," Belinda agreed. "But I think you might be too attached to your bugs if you name them all."

"Hey, Tamika!" Charlie yelled from two rows behind us. "Are you going to name one after me?"

"I'm saving your name for the ugliest one," she replied, and everyone laughed. Oscar laughed the loudest.

Charlie grinned. "I'll be famous. Tamika, you're too kind. We should share the honor."

She just rolled her eyes.

Brakes squealing, the school bus pulled to a stop at my street corner. As the doors whooshed open, Belinda promised to call me later. We were going on a bug hunt.

Dry brown leaves swirled around me. It was the first week of October and still warm. But that's the way the weather always is in Houston.

As I walked four doors down to my house, I noticed the garage door was open. That meant

Mom had been painting her ceramics for the upcoming craft shows.

I peeked inside the garage. No sign of Mom. The front door slammed as Alexander, my little brother, ran outside, a paper bag clutched in one hand. He paused uncertainly when he saw me, then waved.

"Hi, Meggie," he called. Then he dashed across the yard to our neighbor's house.

"Mom, I'm home," I yelled as I came in and started up the stairs to my room.

My bedroom door was open. I never, ever, leave it open.

Someone had been in my room.

Not Mom, because she respects my privacy and I'm supposed to clean my own room.

Not Dad, because he goes to work before I leave for school and doesn't come home until after six.

Alexander.

Taking a deep breath, I walked into my room.

And then I saw it.

chapter

2

My corkboard was empty.

Of all the insects that I had carefully pinned and labeled, not a single one remained. Gone was the giant moth I'd found dead near the porch light. Gone were the mosquito and the ant. Gone was the wasp my mother had sprayed—and practically drowned—with hairspray in her bedroom.

I stood speechless, staring at my ruined science project. I'd have to start all over again. And I only had a few weeks until it was due.

A scream that started from deep within me welled to the surface.

"Mom!"

Racing downstairs I almost collided with my mother as she hurried out of her bedroom.

"What's wrong? What happened?"

"Alexander stole all my bugs!"

"Oh. I thought you'd been hurt." She visibly relaxed and began rubbing paint from the knuckles on her left hand.

"I *am* hurt! How am I going to find twenty-five insects in two weeks?"

She smiled. "Goodness, I don't think we have a bug shortage."

"Mom," I pleaded, "when's Dad getting a lock for my door? I need a way to keep Alexander out of my things."

"Your father's been meaning to do something about that," she said. "It's just that we've both been so busy. . . ."

That was the problem—they were *always* busy. I started out the door.

"Where are you going, sweetheart?"

"Next door. Maybe I can still find Alexander— and my bugs."

Mom followed me as I raced to our neighbor's house where my brother's best friend lived.

Alexander and Jerome knelt in the dirt under

the oak tree in the backyard, gardening spades in their hands.

"Alexander, where—are—my—insects?"

My brother turned a dirt-streaked face up to me. Shaggy brown locks hung in his eyes. "Hi, Meggie. Me and Jerome buried them."

"You *buried* my bugs?"

Jerome nodded solemnly and held up a tiny cross made of two toothpicks glued together. "We had a funeral for them."

Behind him I could see several more crosses. Jerome jabbed a cross into the dirt.

Mom knelt next to Alexander and put her arm around him. "That's so sweet."

"Sweet?" I rolled my eyes. "Mother! That was my science project!"

She looked up at me. "I know, dear, but look at all this. Can't you find some more bugs?" Her eyes begged me.

Ignoring her, I yelled, "Alexander, dig up my insects right this minute!"

Tears squeezed out of his eyes and rolled down his dirty cheek. "But, Meggie, those bugs are *dead*. We had to bury them."

I knew he wasn't faking it. Those were real

tears, because my five-year-old brother sincerely loved all bugs.

So, no longer yelling, I tried to speak in a normal tone. "I need those insects for my homework, Alexander. And I need for them to be dead. You have to stop messing with my things."

He snuffled and wiped his wet cheek on his shirtsleeve, smearing it. "That poor little wasp died with his wings stuck together. He couldn't . . . couldn't . . . even fly home." His eyes, as sad as a cocker spaniel's, brimmed with fresh tears.

I couldn't help it. My heart softened, and I sighed.

He's the only kid I know who has bug books, toy bugs, bug puppets, and posters of bugs decorating his room. He could tell you anything you wanted to know about bugs. In our house if we killed a bug, we had to do it without Alexander knowing. Otherwise, he'd cry. Just like now.

"Okay," I said, giving in. "Those insects can stay buried. But, Alexander, from now on you have to stay out of my room. I mean it!"

He nodded, then patted one of the mounds. "Poor little bugs."

"Poor little me," I muttered.

Mom smiled up at me. "Thank you, Megan, for being so understanding."

Understanding? I would never, ever, understand how someone could weep over a dead wasp or mosquito. And I doubted if I'd ever understand anything about my brother.

I left them there and ran back to call Belinda. "It's an emergency," I said, then told her what Alexander had done.

She laughed hard, not even trying to hide her amusement. "You could always tell Mrs. Tennyson your brother buried your homework."

I snorted. "She wouldn't believe me."

"You'll have to show me Alexander's bug cemetery later. You might have a tourist attraction on your hands."

Her humor was rubbing off on me. "Well, I'll give you the first official tour tonight when you come over."

"I'll be there after dinner, and I'll bring a flashlight."

"Hmmm. What should I charge?"

Belinda giggled. "I'll pay you in bugs. Right now that's worth more than money."

I felt a little better after hanging up the phone. I tried to do some homework but couldn't concentrate. My mind was full of bugs . . . how to catch them—and how to keep them. Finally I gave up and went outside.

Alexander and Jerome had finished with their funeral services and were now climbing a tree. I sneaked around to the front porch, so Alexander wouldn't see me. It was too soon to face him.

Dad was working late tonight, so he wouldn't have time to fix my door. If I wanted it done, I'd have to do it myself.

But how? Without a lock, even my new insects wouldn't be safe.

I racked my brain. My bike came with a chain and combination lock. Maybe there was a way to attach the chain to the doorjamb and to my door, and then chain my door closed during the day. It sounded hard.

A mosquito buzzed in my ear, and I automatically slapped it. It squished in my hand. I should have tried to catch it! The sun was setting, and crickets were beginning to chirp.

One actually hopped near me. I sat very still and watched it, willing it to come closer. It stood motionless. Then it leaped, landing near my leg. I was going to have to catch this thing with my bare hands, without anything to put it in. I'd do it for science.

The cricket studied my leg for a moment, then turned itself around. As it started to leap once more, I cupped my hands together and scooped it up.

It tickled the palm of my hand, but I didn't even care. I spread my fingers apart just a fraction, so it wouldn't get squished.

My next problem was getting it inside and into a jar—without using my hands.

Keeping my hands cupped together, I pushed myself up with my elbows. There was a rustle behind me.

"What do you got in your hand, Meggie?"

Startled, I whirled around. My fingers opened a tiny bit. A tiny bit too much.

chapter 3

The cricket leaped for freedom. I clutched at air as it landed on the porch.

"Oh, a cricket!" Alexander exclaimed. He grabbed at it but missed.

I chased it into a corner. It hopped to one side. Alexander reached down and grabbed it.

"Thanks for catching the cricket," I said, holding out my hands.

He turned away from me and spoke to the cricket. "You can be my pet," he told it.

"Give it back," I said, using the meanest face I could manage. "That's *my* cricket."

He shook his head, holding the cricket close to his chest. "I caught him, Meggie."

"But I caught him first!"

"You dropped him."

Leaning close to his face, I emphasized each word. "Give—it—back."

"But, Meggie," he said, his eyes welling up with tears, "you just want to kill him." Then he started bawling.

Mom raced through the front door, then scooped up my brother as fast as Alexander had scooped up my cricket. "My poor baby," she cooed. "Are you hurt?"

"Nooo." He gulped in air, then stuttered as the sobs interrupted his words. "Meggie . . . is gonna . . . kill . . . my pet."

"Megan!" Mom looked truly horrified.

"That's not his pet," I protested. "It's *my* cricket."

Mom sighed, sounding impatient. "How am I ever going to get dinner on the table with you two arguing? Megan, please don't fight with your baby brother over a cricket."

"He's not a baby, and I caught it first."

"But, Meggie," Alexander said, his crying finished, "you dropped it, and then I caught it."

"It's for my science project!"

"He's only five years old, Megan." Mom

brushed shaggy hair back from Alexander's fore-head. "He doesn't understand about things like science projects. Don't you think you can find another cricket, honey?"

"Mom, it's not that easy. They're hard to catch."

"I'm sure you can catch another one, okay, Megan? It sounds like there're plenty of them out in the yard." She gave me a pleading look, then opened the door with her free hand. Alexander straddled her hip, like he'd done since he was an infant. "Let's find a jar for your bug," she told him.

As they walked into the house, I could hear my brother saying, "I named him Cricky, because he's a field cricket. And he's a boy. I know, because only boy crickets can sing. We can feed him lettuce and bread and water."

Then the door closed, and I couldn't hear them anymore. Just as well.

I stayed sitting on the porch, my chin in my hands. There had to be a way to catch insects without my brother knowing about it. Otherwise, he'd just claim them all. And obviously my mother would let him.

Life was so unfair.

Dinner was sloppy joes and Alexander babbling on about his new pet, Cricky. I had to admit he knew much more about crickets than I did. The Discovery Channel, I guess. And Mom did read a lot of bug books to him.

I tried not to sigh too loudly as Alexander went from crickets to a bug I'd never heard of before. The giant wetapunga that lives in New Zealand is some kind of cricket cousin. Great dinner conversation.

"They only come out at night and eat berries," my brother said. "Mom, could Cricky and me go to New Zealand to visit one of his cousins?"

I couldn't help it. I laughed out loud as Mom tried to hide her smile. Alexander may have been our insect expert, but he had no clue about geography.

Finally Belinda came to save me. We headed outside with our flashlights and several containers to hold our catches.

"All that kid does is cry and he gets his way," I complained as soon as I was out of Mom's hearing. "If I tried that tactic, my parents would just say, 'Grow up.' But they don't say it to Alexander. When does *he* have to grow up?"

Belinda nodded sympathetically, then panned the beam of her flashlight around the front yard. "Come out, come out, wherever you are, little buggies."

I switched on my flashlight and swept the beam down on the grass. No insects. Where were the crickets? Had we scared them away?

Soft yellow light pooled at the base of the streetlight, rippling faintly outward. Things were flying around the metal pole. Insect things, I hoped.

"This way," I said to Belinda.

"We hit the jackpot!" Belinda leaped around me in a little dance.

"Watch out," I teased. "You're going to scare them all away."

"My dancing's not that bad."

I laughed. "Trust me. It is. Hey," I shouted, "there's a June bug by your foot. Grab it!"

Belinda picked up the bug between her thumb and index finger. Its spindly legs still scurried in midair as she held it aloft. Then she yelled, flinging it toward me.

"Oh, gross." She wiped her hands down the side of her shorts.

"Why'd you do that?"

"Girl, if you think that was a June bug, you'll flunk science without any help from Alexander!"

"What was it, then?"

She made a face. "First of all, it's not June, in case you haven't noticed. It's October. June bugs . . . June . . . get it?"

I waved her away. "Yeah, yeah, get to the point."

"Second of all, that was a roach. A nasty, hairy cockroach."

"Was it really hairy?"

Grinning, Belinda said, "No, but it really was nasty."

"Well, nasty or not, I could've used it." I looked longingly to the shadows where the bug had disappeared. "I'm the girl with zero insects, remember?"

"Next time *you* get to grab the roach. I've already got a roach for my collection, thank you."

A moth darted around the streetlight, weaving in and out of the light and shadows. Then it landed on the metal pole.

Belinda grabbed at the moth, just missing it. It fluttered and weaved around the streetlight. I leaped after it, also missing.

"Moths are as hard to catch as crickets," I complained.

Belinda ignored me, keeping her eyes on the moth. When it landed once more on the pole, she quietly crept forward, like a cat after a bird. Then she pounced with cupped hands, trapping the moth between her fingers and the metal pole.

"I got it! I got it!" she yelled.

Quickly I held a plastic butter tub up next to her hand. She slowly opened it, brushing the moth down into the tub. I snapped the lid.

We had our first prize of the night.

I caught the next one. Pretty soon we had five moths. We only needed one each, but it wouldn't hurt to have extras. Especially with Alexander around. Maybe I could bribe him to stop bugging me if I gave him a moth as a pet.

Something flew past my ear and pinged on the ground. Belinda and I both turned around, but we couldn't see anything in the darkness. I switched on my flashlight and swept it across my front yard.

Still nothing.

Ping.

I looked near my feet and saw a pebble that

had been thrown at me. Belinda and I both heard a rustling noise. She pointed her flashlight toward the bushes near my driveway. The branches swayed in the breezeless night.

My heart sank. Alexander was supposed to be in bed by now.

"Is it an animal?" Belinda whispered.

"Animals don't throw pebbles. It's just my pesky brother." I marched over to the bush and pushed the branches aside. "Come on out, Alexander."

Two large dark things leaped out.

Two large dark things that weren't my brother. I screamed.

chapter
4

I couldn't believe my eyes.

Two boys dressed in black clothing rolled on the ground, laughing hysterically.

"Did you see her face?" Hector asked, then howled with glee.

Choking back his own laughter, Charlie tried to speak. "I've . . . never seen anything . . . so funny!"

"Well, I have," I said, shining the flashlight on them. "The two of you. What are you, cat burglars?"

This only made them cackle more. I switched off my flashlight and walked back over to Belinda and the streetlight.

She shook her head. "I don't know what's wrong with them."

Finally they pulled themselves together and walked over to where we were standing.

"Oh, man," Hector said to me, "did you think I was a big, bad bug?"

Charlie stopped just outside the pool of light. "Why don't you try to catch us?"

" 'Cause we don't want any stinkbugs," Belinda said. "What are y'all doing here, anyway?"

"Bugging you," Hector said, then collapsed on the ground in another fit of laughter. "I crack myself up."

I rolled my eyes. "Go away."

"We're just having fun with you," Hector said, sitting up. He leaped to his feet and dusted off his jeans. "So, have you caught anything?"

"A few moths," Belinda said.

"How many bugs do you have in all?" Hector leaned lazily against the light pole.

"Thirteen," Belinda said proudly.

Hector thumped his chest. "I've got you beat! I've got sixteen already."

Belinda stuck her tongue out at him. "Boys like bugs. You probably eat them for lunch."

"Yum," Hector said, "they're crunchy."

"Well, I've got no bugs at all, thanks to my stupid little brother." I felt grouchy, remembering Alexander's latest stunt.

"What'd he do?" Charlie asked.

Belinda giggled. "He buried her bugs, and she promised to show me the insect graveyard."

"Now, *that* I have to see," Hector said. "Lead the way."

"No way," I said.

"Aw, come on," he pleaded. "We really want to see it. Don't we, Charlie?"

Charlie shrugged.

I shook my head.

"We're sorry we scared you, Megan," Hector said. "Aren't we, Charlie?"

Again Charlie shrugged.

Again I shook my head.

Hector went down on one knee. "I'm begging you!"

Belinda nudged me. "You promised to show me, why not them?"

"I promised *you*," I said, "not the whole world."

"Only us three," Hector said, "not everybody."

"I thought you were going to charge a bug for admission," Belinda said.

"I'll give you one of my bugs," Hector promised.

I sighed. "Oh, all right. Follow me. But be quiet. It's in my neighbor's backyard."

Switching on my flashlight, I led them through the wooden gate. Charlie was unusually quiet. I figured he'd be the one to yell and make my neighbors run outside. Instead, he hung back from the rest of us.

Belinda and I shone our flashlights at the base of the oak tree. And there in the beams were the tiny toothpick crosses, casting thin dark shadows across the dirt mounds.

"Aw, isn't that cute?" Hector said.

I snorted. "Cute? That's my science project buried six inches under."

"Why can't you just dig them up again?" Belinda asked.

"The shovel would mess up the insects. No broken bugs allowed, remember?"

"You mean your brother didn't make itty-bitty caskets to bury them in?" Hector joked.

"Don't give him any ideas," I said.

Hector knelt on the ground to examine the graves more closely. "Man, that's a shame. What are you going to do? Bring Mrs. Tennyson here to check out the insect cemetery?"

"Yeah, right." I swung my beam of light away from the tiny crosses and headed back toward the gate.

Hector trotted up to me. "I'll give you one of my bugs. That insect graveyard was definitely worth the price of admission. Especially at night. It's cute and creepy at the same time."

I pushed the gate open and held it as the others walked through.

"That's okay," I said. "You don't have to give me one you've already caught. Just catch me a bug tonight."

"Deal," Hector said, then turned to his friend. "Charlie, are you going to catch Megan a bug, too?"

"Naw."

Belinda cocked her head in his direction. "Are you giving her one you've already caught?"

"Naw," he said again. "I haven't caught any."

"Why not?" I asked.

"Don't get him started," Hector complained.

Charlie's brows bunched together as he frowned. "Because it's a stupid assignment. Unless I'm going to be an exterminator, what do I care about catching and killing bugs?"

"But if you don't do it," I said, "you'll fail. It's the major grade of the whole six weeks!"

He shrugged again, a gesture that was driving me crazy. "Who cares?"

"So don't do the assignment," Belinda said. "But you could help Megan find more bugs. *She* wants to pass science, even if you don't."

"Yeah, yeah," Charlie said. But I noticed he didn't really say he'd help me. Fine, I didn't need him, anyway.

We walked back to the streetlight, where moths still fluttered. A small roach skittered near Hector's foot.

Hector chased it, running in circles and zigzags as he tried to catch it. The rest of us laughed as we watched him. Finally he got close enough and scooped it up. We burst into applause, whistling and cheering, too.

"Hey, I got it!" he yelled.

"Normally I hate those things," I said, wrinkling my nose. "But tonight it looks pretty good."

Hector held it up to the streetlight, admiring it. "Not bad for a roach. Kind of small, though, next to Tamika's."

"It'll do for me," I told him. "Tamika needs to send hers to the *Guinness Book of World Records.*"

"Here, check out your very own bug," Hector said, dangling it right in my face.

"Thanks." I snatched it from him. The roach wiggled and squirmed in my cupped hand. Only a couple of months ago I never would have held a roach. Now I was grabbing them from people!

"Oh, cool!" Belinda yelled. "Look at this twig with legs!"

"Wow!" Hector ran over to where Belinda stood near the street lamp. "I haven't seen a walking stick in a long time."

I had my hands full of wriggling roach, so I didn't join them. I bent down to pick up a butter tub and collided with Charlie.

My hand, holding the roach, whacked him in the chest. Charlie's eyes widened as he jumped sideways. He brushed vigorously at his shirt.

"Is it on me?" Charlie kept wiping at his clothes.

"No, I still have it." I held out my hand to show him.

Charlie's hands stilled, and he glanced up at me. "Uh, is it still in one piece?"

"Yeah," I said. I was getting suspicious.

Just then Charlie gave me a smile. "I sure don't want to hurt your roach. You need all the help you can get."

Now, that sounded like Charlie.

"Boy, do I," I said. "Could you hand me that butter tub? I have to put my bug in something before it gets away."

Charlie reached down and picked up the one near his foot, then removed the opaque lid.

A moth flew out, fluttering near his face.

Charlie yelped as he dropped the container.

And that's when I knew for sure.

chapter 5

Charlie looked me straight in the eye. He knew I'd figured it out.

"A little jumpy tonight, aren't we?" I commented.

Charlie scowled. "Why didn't you tell me there was already a bug in there?"

"I didn't know you'd pick that one," I said carefully. "You're acting kind of upset."

He shrugged. "Who's upset?"

I started to say something, then changed my mind. "Nobody."

Charlie handed me the empty butter tub, and I put my cockroach inside.

Did Hector know? He was Charlie's best

friend. Could he be covering for Charlie? But Hector and Belinda weren't nearby. I was the only one who had seen Charlie's reaction to the roach and moth.

No matter how hard it might be to believe, it had to be true. Charlie Bettencourt, the boy nothing bothered, was afraid of bugs.

I didn't think he was pretending. Otherwise, why wouldn't he have collected *any* insects for his science project?

That meant there was no way he'd help me find more insects, not if he wouldn't even find them for himself. Well, I wasn't going to help him, either. If he failed, he failed. His problem, not mine.

My problem was keeping the bugs we captured tonight away from Alexander.

By the time Belinda's mother came to pick her up, I had three moths, a roach, a mosquito, and some kind of beetle no one recognized. I guess I'd have to go to the library and look it up.

Belinda added a moth to her collection, as well as a mosquito and a really cool walking stick. She only needed nine more insects. I needed twenty-one and the witness protection program to keep their identities secret from my brother.

Hector and an unusually quiet Charlie left without any bugs. They didn't want any. Hector already had a moth, a mosquito, a roach, a beetle, and a fly. Charlie had nothing and insisted he didn't care.

Now I had to find a way to kill my insects without damaging them. Mrs. Tennyson had said we could put them in a jar without airholes or put a drop of nail polish remover in the jar to suffocate them, or put them in the freezer. The freezer sounded like a good idea, because Alexander would definitely find a jar of bugs in my room. Out of sight, out of Alexander's mind.

When I went inside, Alexander was already in bed. My parents were engrossed in a TV movie in the family room. I put the butter tubs in the freezer—except one. That was the moth I planned to bribe Alexander with so he'd leave the others alone. I punched airholes in the lid and brought it to my room.

I went to bed feeling pretty good about my insects.

The next morning Mom shook me awake. Only inches away her face glowered at mine.

"What is going on in my refrigerator?" she demanded, tapping her left foot.

Raising up on my elbows, I blinked sleepy eyes at her. "Is this a trick question?"

"The only trick is if you can successfully answer my question without getting into trouble."

I sat up and scratched my scalp. It felt itchy after last night's bug hunt. "Wait a minute," I said. "Do you mean the refrigerator or the freezer?"

"The freezer section of my refrigerator." Mom crossed her arms in front of her chest. "So you *do* know what I'm talking about."

I yawned. "Those are my bugs we caught last night."

"And why are they in the freezer?"

"To kill them."

"In my freezer?"

"Yeah," I said. "I didn't want Alexander to find them."

"So you hid them in my freezer."

I looked at her, puzzled. "What's wrong with that?"

"Oh, nothing," Mom said, switching her tapping to her right foot—a sure sign that something was wrong. "I was just getting out the ice trays to make orange juice when I accidentally knocked out a butter tub. A tub I knew *I* hadn't put there. A tub that fell to the floor and popped open at my feet." She paused for dramatic effect. "A tub with a roach in it that fell on my foot."

"Is the roach all right?" By the angry look in my mother's eyes, I knew that had been the wrong question to ask.

"The roach! Young lady, march down there and clean up the mess I made when I screamed and threw ice cubes all over the kitchen."

It could have been worse. It could have been something sticky. But I still had to mop the kitchen floor before school.

The roach was ruined. Mom had stomped on it, not realizing it was already dead. Alexander gathered the remains to be buried later in the insect graveyard.

Before I left for school, I presented the surviving moth to Alexander. He accepted it gravely.

"Thank you, Meggie," he said. "I'll name her Motha and take good care of her."

Cute name, I thought. Better than Cricky. "Okay," I said, "you understand that you have to leave my dead insects alone. I'm giving you a live moth so that you won't touch my dead moth."

He nodded, shaggy hair bouncing around his ears.

"And you'll stay out of my room?"

Again he nodded. "I promise."

I smiled as I left the house for the school bus. The morning had started off badly, but I'd convinced Mom to let me keep the insects in the freezer. I promised to label the butter tubs and to let her know whenever I added another one. That seemed reasonable. And best of all, Alexander had promised to stay out of my room!

"You're pretty cheery this morning," Belinda said as I slid onto the bench seat beside her.

The school bus rumbled along, bouncing us as it hit a pothole. I told her about the bugs in the freezer and Alexander's promise.

Belinda laughed and clutched her side. "The funniest things happen at your house."

I rolled my eyes. "I don't think they're so funny."

"Give me a break. I would've loved to have seen your mom's face this morning. Bugs for breakfast!" That set her off again.

"Well, I saw Mom's face up close this morning,

and it wasn't a pretty sight. She must have been petrified when she saw that roach!" That reminded me. "By the way, did you notice how funny Charlie acted last night?"

"Yeah, he must really like you. He sure was being goofy." Belinda stole a glance behind her to where Charlie and his friends were shooting spitballs at each other. It took more than flying spitballs to make our bus driver react.

"I don't think that's the reason—"

"Of course it is," Belinda interrupted me. "Don't deny it."

"I don't like Charlie, and he doesn't like me. But I do think he's afraid of insects."

"Insects!" Belinda giggled. "Boy, are you crazy!"

"He hasn't collected a single bug for his assignment and doesn't plan on it in the future. Sounds to me like maybe he isn't too fond of bugs."

"Like Charlie does all his homework all the time?" Belinda shook her head. "It won't work, Megan. You can't make up stuff like that to change the subject. You just don't want to admit it. Charlie likes you a lot. Trust me, I can tell."

"If he likes me, then why didn't he help me last night?"

"Can't you see it? You had him flustered." She giggled. "He looked embarrassed half the time, even in the dark."

This argument wasn't going anywhere. I wasn't going to convince Belinda of anything . . . at least not this morning. It was strange, Charlie and Hector showing up like that last night, but they only lived a few blocks from me. And last night I could have sworn he was afraid of bugs, but now I wasn't so sure. Who knew? Maybe Belinda was right about Charlie liking me.

As we were getting off the bus, Charlie passed me. "Well, if it isn't Beggin' Megan. You still begging for bugs?" Before I could say anything, he turned back to everyone crowding to the front of the bus. "Hey, if anybody has a spare bug, give it to Megan. She's begging, pleeeeasssse!" The last word was said in a high-pitched wail.

Everyone laughed, and I could feel my face turning red.

This is the way a boy acts when he's supposed to like you? No thank you!

I turned and marched off the bus, ignoring the chants of "Beggin' Megan."

As we waded through the sea of kids trying to get to their lockers before class, I said, "So much for your theory of Charlie liking me."

"Oh, he was just teasing. Boys do that when they like you."

I snorted. "Then he must *really* like Oscar."

We stood in front of our lockers. "It's not the same," Belinda said, stuffing her backpack inside her locker.

I merely raised my eyebrows.

History was my first class, but Belinda wasn't in it. She waved as she headed down a different hallway.

Mrs. Matzke hadn't arrived in the classroom yet.

But Charlie had.

He stood at the blackboard, writing something in large letters.

I felt my heart sink.

He was writing about me.

chapter

6

I slumped down into my seat. In large white letters Charlie had written:

BEGGIN' MEGAN IS BEGGING FOR BUGS!
Please donate your extra bugs. Any kind!
Check your lockers, your backpacks, your lunch.
It's for a good cause.
Sponsored by the Society
for the Insect–Catching Impaired.
Call Megan Hollander,
President of SICI, at 555-3481.
SHE'S BEGGING!

Charlie dusted off his hands and sat down, a pleased expression on his face. The class burst into laughter as they read the blackboard.

Stomping up to the front of the room, I grabbed an eraser. Mrs. Matzke chose that moment to make her entrance.

My hand froze before I could take the first swipe at the board. Mrs. Matzke stood silently, hands on hips, frown on face, reading the board.

"Very interesting, Megan. Perhaps you'd like to discuss this with me after school?"

Tamika saved me. "Megan didn't write that, Mrs. M. Charlie Bettencourt was just trying to be funny."

Mrs. Matzke raised her eyebrows at him. "Is this true?"

Charlie showed his dimples as he grinned. "I guess you don't think it's funny?"

She smiled. "You and I can discuss your humor after school, all right?"

"Yes, ma'am." He still grinned, as if he stayed after school every day to talk to Mrs. Matzke. Maybe he did. In detention.

Lenora Bell, who majored in being the teacher's pet, raised her hand. "I just want you to know, Mrs. Matzke, there are a few of us who take our homework seriously."

Mrs. Matzke smiled, the class groaned, and Charlie grinned at me. He mouthed the word pleeeeasssse. I rolled my eyes.

The day went downhill after that. Charlie talked about me in all his classes, telling everyone how badly I needed bugs. Now, that *sounds* like a nice thing to do. But not the way Charlie was doing it. He made it sound stupid, as if I were a total moron who couldn't catch an insect if my life depended on it. He made everyone laugh about it. Now no one took my plight seriously.

At lunch Charlie made a big display of checking his hamburger for bugs. "I'm doing this for Beggin' Megan," he declared.

Soon he had everyone laughing about it as if it were the greatest joke ever.

"And you said he liked me." I poked Belinda as she took a bite of her turkey sandwich.

"Boys are stupid." She chewed thoughtfully.

"Tell me something I don't know. Like how am I ever going to get enough bugs?"

She shrugged as she swallowed. "I don't have

enough bugs, either. And I don't have a dopey brother who steals them."

"And buries them," I reminded her.

"My two little sisters shriek and run away whenever they see my collection," Belinda continued. "My older sister says, 'Yeah, I remember doing that project,' but she hasn't offered to help." She took another bite and said, "I don't know, Megan. Sneaking into the cafeteria's kitchen doesn't sound so crazy anymore."

"Forget it. Let's just go on another bug hunt after school."

"Day or night?"

"Day this time."

She licked mustard off her fingers. "The problem is the later in the year it gets, the harder it is to find bugs. They all hibernate or something. Maybe they fly south for the winter."

"Maybe they pack tiny suitcases and get tiny sunglasses and go to Mexico." I giggled.

Belinda did, too. "You could always tell Mrs. Tennyson, 'Gee, I'm sorry I couldn't do my assignment, but all the bugs are vacationing in Acapulco.'"

"At a roach motel!"

We had English class after lunch. Charlie was waiting by the door. I started to walk by, but he stopped us.

"Go away, Charlie," I said. "Haven't you done enough?"

"Why, Megan, am I bugging you?" He sounded so innocent.

"Yes! Go away!"

He ignored me and turned to Belinda. "Knock, knock."

She rolled her eyes heavenward, but said, "Okay, I'll play your game. Who's there?"

"Donut."

"Donut who?"

In a shrill voice, he said, "Donut bug me!" He elbowed Belinda as he waggled his eyebrows. "Get it? Don't bug me! I'm pretending to be Megan."

"Very funny," Belinda said, and followed me into the classroom.

"Boys aren't stupid," I said. "They're jerks."

"Well, Charlie's sure acting like one."

I pulled out my textbook. "So what am I going to do about it? I don't think he's going to stop any time soon."

"I can't believe how much he's teasing you.

And I thought he really liked you." She sighed. "Ignore him, I guess."

"He's hard to ignore."

Belinda leaned back in her chair. "I don't know what else to tell you. I'm out of ideas."

"All right. I'll try ignoring him and maybe he'll go away, or at least get tired of making fun of me."

The rest of the day I tried to ignore him. The problem was that everyone thought Charlie's knock-knock joke was hysterical, and they were repeating it endlessly. I didn't think it was the least bit funny.

In class and in the halls I had lots of offers of bugs, but I knew that none was serious. When someone can't stop laughing as he's making the offer, I don't think it's an offer I can count on.

On the bus Charlie told jokes and riddles all having to do with my bug shortage. "Have you heard of Megan Math?" he asked the busload of kids. "You can only subtract bugs, never add."

I was getting sick and tired of it. When the bus stopped on my street, I was already at the doors, waiting for them to open.

Belinda called after me as I fled down the steps, "See you later for a bug hunt."

That remark caused gales of laughter. She

didn't mean to do it, but it was more than I could bear. I ran down the street to my house.

Oooh, that Charlie Bettencourt! What had I ever done to him?

Nothing!

Well, nothing except discover his secret.

But I hadn't told anyone!

Well, no one except Belinda, who didn't believe me anyway.

Still, he had no right to make fun of me all day. Now I knew exactly how Oscar felt. Except today Oscar had been laughing just as loudly as everyone else. Great. Just great!

A few deep breaths calmed me down. My mind needed to be off Charlie and on my homework. Belinda was coming over soon. We'd need more butter tubs, so I headed for the kitchen.

Kneeling on a chair at the breakfast table, Alexander bent over the tabletop and closely studied the contents of three butter tubs.

My butter tubs!

chapter

7

"What are you doing?" I screamed.

My brother must have jumped two feet. He turned in the chair and said warily, "Uh, hi, Meggie."

I rushed to the table to claim my defrosting insects. "You promised," I yelled. "You promised not to touch any of my bugs!"

Alexander looked confused. "But Meggie, I didn't touch your *dead* bugs. These bugs are *frozen*. Why did you put them in the freezer?"

"To kill them!" I snatched the butter tubs from the table and inspected the insects closely.

His confusion turned to horror. "You *killed* them? In the freezer?"

I was exasperated. How could he not know? "Of course. What'd you think?"

Alexander's eyes got all watery.

Uh-oh, here we go again. I knew one thing my brother would never be when he grew up. An exterminator. He'd weep all over some little old lady's roach-infested kitchen and then carry the icky things home to be pets.

"Poor little buggies." He sniffed and wiped his eyes.

Sighing, I pulled him over to stand in front of me. "Now, look, Alexander, you have to stop crying. I mean, you can't cry every time a bug dies."

"But we cried when Fluffy died," he said.

"Fluffy was our cat. That's different."

"Why?"

Where was Mom when I needed her? "Because Fluffy was our pet. We loved her. Bugs are not supposed to be pets."

He looked up at me, sad eyes awash with tears. "Bugs are my pets. I love them."

"Not every bug is your pet. Besides, insects are yucky."

"Moths aren't yucky," Alexander said. "They're pretty."

"Moths eat wool clothing," I countered. "And crickets eat crops."

"Crickets sing me to sleep," he said.

"What about June bugs? They're stupid," I said, "flying around crazily and bumping into everything."

"They make me laugh."

"What about roaches?" I challenged. "They're really nasty."

"Well, maybe." He thought for a moment. "But roaches have lasted even longer than dinosaurs."

This argument was going nowhere. I threw up my hands in frustration.

"And what about butterflies?" he asked me. "They're the prettiest bugs ever. Butterflies and ladybugs are my favorites." He got teary-eyed again and wiped his nose on his shirt. "And you want to kill them."

"I've never killed a bug that you claimed as a pet. You know that."

He nodded. "And you gave me Motha."

"That's right. And the bugs I catch are part of my homework assignment for science. I've told you that before. Now you have to stop touching any of my bugs, dead, alive, or frozen." I held out my hand. "You promise?"

"I promise." He said it reluctantly, but he took my hand and we shook. In my heart I knew he didn't understand that I needed the insects for my homework. But I didn't know how to explain it to him.

Luckily the insects looked okay. I guess Alexander had just been looking at them as he'd claimed. I snapped the lids on the butter tubs and tucked them back in the freezer until I was ready to pin them.

Belinda walked in the door as Alexander ran outside to play with Jerome. She had a handful of plastic bags and held them up for me to see.

"My bug-hunting equipment," she said, following me back into the kitchen.

I opened a cabinet door and a bunch of butter tubs fell out. "I'm glad my mother saves these. They work pretty well."

"Why does she save them?"

I shrugged. "For holding ceramic paint or brush cleaner. Or leftovers that turn green and moldy in the back of the refrigerator."

Belinda giggled. "Sounds like our refrigerator . . . a regular science experiment."

We headed outside with our bags and tubs, ready to catch some creepy, crawly things. And we actually had some luck! We found some ladybugs that really did look cute. I could see why Alexander liked them. They crawled all over our hands as we checked out their black-and-red designs.

"Look," Belinda said, kneeling beside a mound of loose dirt. "An ant bed! Ants are easy to catch."

"If it's so easy," I asked, "then how do we do it?"

Belinda opened a butter tub and scooped the top of the mound into it. "There's bound to be some ants in the dirt."

As we bent over the tub to count the ants, the dirt mound beside us erupted like a volcano. Ants poured out, ready to defend their home against the giant attackers. Suddenly we were surrounded.

I jumped aside and brushed a couple of ants off my sneakers. But Belinda was still kneeling next to the mound. By the time she leaped up, she was kicking her feet higher than the high school drill team.

"Fire ants!" she yelled as she swatted at her legs. She twirled and kicked some more, then she shook all over.

I started laughing. I couldn't help it. She just looked so funny! I tried to help her, but she danced away from me.

"I've got ants in my pants," she screeched. She twisted and turned and leaped up and down.

I staggered backward and fell down in the grass. The muscles in my stomach hurt from laughing.

Belinda collapsed next to me. I examined her legs but only found a couple of ants on her shoes.

"Uh," I said, trying not to giggle, "you want to check your pants?"

"No!" Belinda huffed and puffed. "I think they're gone now."

"I should think so, after all that dancing!"

"Don't you dare say a word tomorrow at school," she warned.

That started me laughing all over again. "What do you suppose Charlie would say about that? Can't you just see his latest message on the chalkboard?"

She gave me a little shove but started

giggling, too. Catching insects was definitely more fun with a friend.

A butterfly flitted by and we chased it, flapping our arms around the yard. Alexander would have been glad. It was safe from us. There was no way we could catch it without a net.

We walked down the street a few houses. Belinda suddenly stopped and pointed.

"That's a cicada!"

I frowned and looked at the base of the tree where she was pointing. An insect with a stout body, wide head, and green transparent wings lay there, dead. "Are you sure?" I asked.

"Yeah." She squatted, then put her hand inside a plastic bag and picked up the cicada. "I remember my older sister had one in her bug collection for school." As she peeled the bag off her hand, still holding the insect, the bag turned inside out. Now the bag held the cicada, and Belinda hadn't touched it with her bare hand.

"Neat trick! Where'd you learn that?"

"My sister." She handed me the bag. "For you, my friend who's begging for bugs."

"That 'begging' part sounds better coming from you."

"What can I say? Love makes people act crazy. And Charlie must be crazy about you."

"Love?" I shuddered. "Give me a break. It's not even 'like.' He doesn't like me—and I sure don't like him."

We walked by a field that had been recently cut. Grasshoppers jumped above the short grass and weeds. Belinda raced across the field, stirring up the grasshoppers, making them leap and fly in all directions. I chased after her, and together we ran around trying to catch at least one.

Finally Belinda pounced—and caught one! Panting, she sat down in the middle of the field to admire it.

"Boy," she said, wiping sweat from her forehead, "bug catching is hard work."

I examined today's collection. We each had an ant and a ladybug. I had a cicada and she had a grasshopper.

"A lot of hard work for not a lot of bugs." I sighed.

"Well, it's better than what we had before." She put the grasshopper into a butter tub and snapped the lid in place.

"At this rate I'll never get enough bugs," I wailed.

"Don't remind me." Belinda lay back on the grass, her hands folded under her head like a pillow. "There's got to be a better way."

"Or at least an easier way," I said. "Like getting bugs from the cafeteria kitchen. There're probably dozens of different kinds hiding out in the cupboards."

"Or hiding in our food," Belinda said. We both pretended to gag.

I looked down at my three bugs, my catch for the day. I also had three in the freezer. "I'm just about desperate enough to try it."

She tilted her head to one side. "Try what?"

"You know, breaking into the cafeteria kitchen."

"But I thought you were kidding."

"Well, I'm not. I need more bugs."

Belinda looked surprised. "Are you serious? About breaking in?"

"Look," I said, "we've got . . . What? Less than two weeks to complete this assignment? The weather's getting cooler, and there are fewer bugs every day. Time—and bugs—are running out. I've got to do something drastic."

She was silent, tapping her chin thoughtfully. "Yeah, you're right," she finally said. "How about tomorrow?"

"The sooner the better."

"Okay, let's do it after school."

"And we can hide in the P.E. lockers until everyone's gone."

Belinda raised her eyebrows. "So P.E. *is* good for something."

"We can hide our equipment in the lockers, too."

"Equipment? Sounds like we're doing a top secret operation."

"Operating Bug Hunt," I said.

We giggled, then got serious as we planned what we needed. Flashlights, bags, tubs, soft-soled shoes—and lots of courage.

Before Belinda went home, we shook on it.

chapter
8

"Oh, yuck! What's that?" Rita pushed the bean soup away from her.

"That's just a bean." Tamika peered closer into the bowl. Something round and dark floated near the surface. "Or it might be a bug."

Several of us crowded around Tamika at one end of the long cafeteria table. Lunch had just started, and Belinda and I had planned to go over Operation Bug Hunt while we ate. Now it looked as if the bug hunt had already begun. We nudged each other.

"What's a bug doing in my soup?" Rita asked.

"The backstroke!" Charlie yelled, and all the boys hooted with laughter.

I pretended to yawn. "That's so old, it's stupid."

My comment didn't bother Charlie. "Right," he said, "it's as old as the hills and twice as dusty." The boys seemed to think this was even more hilarious.

We girls just looked at each other and rolled our eyes. Boys were so immature.

"That was so funny, I forgot to laugh," I said, and plopped my lunch bag onto the table.

Rita used a spoon to fish out the offending object. "I think it's just a bean. . . . No, it *is* a bug!"

Several girls shrieked. Tamika dived for it. Soup sloshed everywhere. Belinda and I grabbed our lunch bags. In the end Rita's soup covered the table like a tablecloth, and Tamika clutched a bug in her hand.

Slowly she opened her fingers. She examined the insect closely. Then she got this really annoyed look on her face.

"Did you take a bite out of it?" Joe Davis yelled, making the boys snort and nudge each other.

"So what kind is it?" Peter asked. Oscar laughed and choked on his milk.

Tamika dropped the bug on the table. "It's fake. It's nothing but a fake plastic beetle." She turned to the boys. "Okay, which one of y'all did this?"

"Yes," said a deep male voice, "I'd like to know that, too."

We all turned around and stared at Mr. Weis, the assistant principal. I guess we'd caused a bit of a commotion. He stood there frowning, arms crossed. Not a good sign.

Rita tried to explain about the bug in her soup, but we kept interrupting her with our own comments. Mr. Weis rubbed his forehead as if he were getting a headache, then motioned for us to stop talking.

"I just want to know who did this," he said.

At first no one said anything, but we girls all looked over at the boys.

Mr. Weis looked sternly at Charlie. "What can you tell me about this, Mr. Bettencourt?"

"Nothing," Charlie said.

Secretly I thought Charlie could probably tell Mr. Weis a lot about the bug in Rita's soup. But I was surprised, after all of Charlie's teasing about bugs, that he put it in Rita's soup and not mine. Maybe he liked Rita now.

"Charlie," the assistant principal said, "tell me the truth. Did you do this?"

"No, sir."

"Then who did?"

Once again no one answered.

Turning to Hector, Mr. Weis asked, "Do *you* know?"

Hector rubbed his chin and looked thoughtful. "I guess I wasn't paying attention. I was, uh, busy eating my lunch." He rubbed his stomach. "And, man, is it goooood!"

Mr. Weis smiled, but it didn't reach his eyes. "Then I guess everyone at this table will get D-Hall."

D-Hall! That's detention. That's school prison! That's totally unfair! Ooooh, that Charlie Bettencourt! He should just admit it, instead of getting us all in trouble.

Oscar spoke up, his face turning positively scarlet. "It was me, Mr. Weis."

We were all stunned. *Oscar?*

"Come with me," Mr. Weis said as he picked up the fake beetle from the table. He tucked the plastic insect into his jacket pocket.

As Oscar stood up, Charlie muttered, "Uh, sir, I dared him to do it."

Ha! I knew Charlie had been in on it somehow!

But I had to admit I was amazed that he confessed when he could have gotten off scot-free.

Mr. Weis paused for a moment. "Charlie, it wasn't very smart to dare someone, but you didn't make him do it. That was Oscar's decision, however unwise. And he is the one who must suffer the consequences of his actions."

With that Mr. Weis turned, put a restraining hand on Oscar's shoulder, and marched him out of the lunchroom.

We all sat back down at the table. One of the cafeteria ladies had come over while Mr. Weis was talking to us, and she mopped up the spilled soup. Belinda and I put our lunch bags back on the table.

"Rita," I said, "Oscar really likes you."

She smiled, her cheeks getting rosy. "I know."

"I can't believe he'd do something so dopey." Belinda pulled her sandwich out of her bag. "I thought Oscar was smarter than that."

Tamika shook her head, making the tight curls bounce. "Those boys are acting plumb crazy. I guess there's just so much teasing a person can stand, and Oscar finally gave in. He could've kissed her, you know."

Belinda wrinkled her nose. "I don't know which would be worse."

"A real bug in my soup, definitely," Rita said, making us all laugh.

The boys, minus Oscar, were clumped together at the other end of the long table, still snickering. They kept poking each other and whispering. Every time they'd look at us, they'd hoot with laughter.

Sixth-grade boys were definitely strange creatures.

All this excitement had made me hungry, and my mother had packed my favorite sandwich: tuna salad. I pulled my lunch bag toward me, then reached inside.

Except, instead of a sandwich, my hand found squishy things. What were they? I grabbed a handful and pulled them out.

And then I screamed!

chapter 9

All the girls started screaming with me. And jumping up and down. And pushing away their food.

There on the table was a mound of dead insects. Squishy dead insects from my lunch bag.

The boys howled. They laughed so hard, they had tears in their eyes. Charlie banged on the table as he hooted. Hector started coughing and cracking up at the same time. Peter shot milk out of his nose, which just made them laugh harder. Joe Davis actually fell out of his seat.

Three cafeteria workers, four teachers, *and* the principal herself ran over to our table. None of them looked the least bit happy.

"What is going on over here?" demanded Mrs. Kopecky, our principal. Her wing-tipped glasses rode the bridge of her nose like an avenging angel on horseback.

"My . . . my lunch," I gasped, "is full of . . . *bugs!*"

This made the boys roar, but the teachers frowned so hard I thought they'd get permanent wrinkles between their eyebrows. Their lips squeezed tight, their eyes narrowed. The cafeteria workers just looked puzzled.

Miss Aznar, our new math teacher, bent close to the table, her blond ponytail flipping forward over her shoulder. She flipped it back, then touched the pile of insects. We all made faces and sort of moaned to ourselves, while thinking how brave she was.

She picked one up and sniffed it, then—to our horror—bit it. We did a group shudder as she smiled.

"It's not real. These are all made of candy. Some kind of gummy bugs." She put the rest of the fake bug in her mouth and chewed as if tasting something heavenly. "Yum. Licorice."

Now what kind of crazy person would even think of making such horrid things? And what kind of person would buy them? Or eat them? Besides Miss Aznar, of course.

I looked over at Charlie.

He was wiping his eyes with one hand and holding his side with the other, as if all that laughter was the best workout he'd ever had.

"It's time to settle down," Mrs. Kopecky said, pushing up her glasses with her index finger. She waited until we sat at the table again. "Now, who did this?"

Charlie looked as if he were about to burst. But he managed to keep it inside as he raised his hand.

"Ah, Charles Bettencourt." She studied him over the top of her glasses. "You've been a busy boy. I've been getting a lot of reports about your activities the last couple of days. You now have the pleasure of telling me all about them. In detail. In my office."

Charlie didn't say a word. He was biting his cheeks, I guess so he wouldn't laugh. He just stood up and followed her out of the room. As soon as the door to the cafeteria closed, even above all the noise, we could hear Charlie explode with laughter. Boy, was he going to get it! He'd have D-Hall for the rest of sixth grade!

"All right, children," said Miss Crowell, our P.E. teacher, "show's over. Eat your lunches." A frown pulled down her plump cheeks, making her look like a bulldog ready to eat *us* for lunch. Instead of a dog collar, she always wore a whistle around her neck.

"Uh, I can't," I said. "All I have is a bag full of candy bugs."

"Me neither," Rita said. "My soup got spilled when we found Oscar's bug in it."

All four teachers sighed deeply in unison. Perhaps they'd been practicing that. Miss Aznar swept the candy bugs back into the bag, grinned at me, and took them with her, her ponytail bouncing behind her. Two of the other teachers and the cafeteria workers left also.

Giving the boys one last glare as they tried not to snicker, Miss Crowell fingered her whistle as she said to us, "All right, come with me. We'll get you something to eat."

Rita and I followed Miss Crowell to the lunch line. I really wasn't looking forward to eating cafeteria food. There'd probably be real bugs in the bean soup this time, but who'd believe us?

After we'd gone through the food line and were back at the table, I whispered to Belinda,

"Do you still want to go through with Operation Bug Hunt?"

She giggled. "Oh yeah. Now more than ever. I bet that kitchen is just crawling with bugs."

I looked down at my bean soup, then pushed it away. "Thanks a lot." I ate my bread and apple instead.

The rest of the day went well, considering the disaster lunch had been. Charlie left me alone, pretty much. But I did catch him and some of the other boys glancing at me and snickering. Probably thinking about how wonderful I looked screaming my head off because of a bag full of candy bugs. Well, I couldn't help it. It was a natural reaction.

As soon as school let out, I met Belinda in the girls' locker room next to the gym. Belinda started to pull out her flashlight, but I stopped her.

"Not here." I looked around. "Wait until we're actually in the kitchen."

She shook off my hand. "It's for when we hide in the lockers. I don't want to be in there a long time in the dark."

"Are you scared of the dark?" I asked, incredulous. "Or are you afraid of small places . . . like lockers?" I swung open the tall narrow door to my locker. "See? It's plenty roomy inside."

"Let's just say that I'm not too thrilled about this part of Operation Bug Hunt."

"We probably won't have to be inside very long," I said. "It kind of depends on the teachers."

Sighing, Belinda nodded. "I know. It'll be another hour and a half before they go home with the late bus."

My breath got stuck in my throat for a moment. "The late bus . . . I completely forgot one important detail of our plan."

"*Now* you tell me your plan isn't perfect?"

"*My* plan? It's *our* plan! And you should have helped me iron out any problems."

"Okay, okay." Belinda frowned. "We've already missed our regular bus, so I guess we're going to be here for a while. Tell me the problem so we can decide if we still want to do Operation Bug Hunt."

"The bus is the problem. How are we going to get home?"

She shrugged. "The late bus."

"That's the problem," I said. "If we take the late bus home, that means we have to sneak into the kitchen *before* all the teachers go home."

Belinda's eyes widened. "That makes it a lot harder."

"If we wait until everyone's gone, we could always walk home."

"That'll take forever, and Mama will wonder why I didn't take the late bus. I told her I was staying for math tutorial. That was easy for her to believe!"

"I told my mother I had to go to a club meeting."

"What? The Science Club?" Belinda giggled.

"Shhh!" I put my finger to my lips, then whispered, "I think I hear somebody coming."

We scurried into our lockers, but I didn't close mine all the way. I held it so it looked closed, but a narrow beam of light crept through. Just enough so that I could see if anyone walked by.

I heard humming, then saw a short, round shadow darken the bench between the rows of lockers.

Miss Crowell!

chapter 10

Miss Crowell hummed off-key as she walked between the rows of lockers. My nose tickled as
I peered at her through the crack. I always
thought that only happened in cartoons and the
movies. But here I was, stuck in a locker and trying not to sneeze.

As quietly as possible, I rubbed my nose and
sniffed. The tickling sensation disappeared.

Miss Crowell stopped humming and paused
in front of my locker. Frowning, she cocked her
head to one side, as if listening for the tiniest
noise.

I held my breath.

If she caught us, she'd be on us like a duck on

a June bug, even if it wasn't June. We'd be deader than the bugs for our science project. She'd think that we really were part of the cafeteria incident, that it wasn't just the boys pulling their usual stunts. Nobody would believe anything I said ever again!

Ohhh, that Charlie Bettencourt!

Apparently satisfied that all was well, Miss Crowell started humming again and walked on down the row. I could no longer see her through the crack in the locker door. Pretty soon I couldn't hear her anymore, either. No footsteps. No humming.

I waited a while longer, wanting to be sure she'd really left. Then I slowly opened the locker door and stepped out.

Boy, was it cramped in there! I knocked softly on Belinda's locker, and she, too, opened the door with care.

Belinda stretched. "I'm glad to be out of that thing! My gym suit is in serious need of washing!"

"We ought to stay here just a little while longer," I whispered. "Make sure the teachers have either left or are settled in their rooms and not roaming the halls."

"As long as I don't have to climb back inside that locker, I'm okay with just staying here." She plopped down on the bench and pulled her knee up to rest her chin on it.

"I don't think we'll have to wait long until we can sneak into the kitchen. Then we'll grab us a bucket of bugs."

Pinching her nose, Belinda said in a nasal voice, "And do you want fries with your bug bucket?"

"Yes, I would. And could you supersize it?"

We both started laughing, and we both tried to hush each other up. But it's impossible to laugh quietly. One of us would snort or hoot really loudly, and that would set the other one off.

"You know what this means, don't you?" I asked.

"That we're getting really silly? Or nervous or something?"

"That too. But we'll never be able to eat cafeteria food again."

"Like it was easy to do that before."

"The good news is we'll go home on the late bus with lots of bugs in our backpacks, and no one will be the wiser."

"Perfect!" She gave me a high five that sounded loud in the large, empty room.

Maybe thirty minutes or more passed before we decided to take a chance and creep out. What a strange feeling! The halls were totally deserted. Every sound echoed. It was almost as if our every tiptoed step were being broadcast over the PA system.

We reached the cafeteria unnoticed and breathed a sigh of relief. All the workers had left. Every day, as soon as the last lunch period is over, they clean the tables and floors and then they leave. Now all the tables and chairs were folded and stacked against a wall. Only one overhead light was on.

"What if they locked the kitchen door?" I whispered.

"Why would they do that? After hours the whole school is locked up."

"The school is locked up?" I put my hand on Belinda's arm. "I just thought of another problem."

"I don't want to hear it."

"You have to!"

She closed her eyes and whispered, "What is it this time?"

"If the whole school is locked up after hours, how are we going to get out?"

"The doors are locked from the outside. From the inside you just push the bar. Besides, we'll just go out with the kids who are staying for the late bus."

I breathed a sigh of relief. "Sorry I panicked. It's just that I'm getting nervous," I whispered.

"Me too."

I followed Belinda through the swinging doors into the large, dark kitchen. My heart pounded and my palms were damp. Sweat beaded on my forehead. I wasn't sure if I was more afraid of getting caught by monster teachers or monster cafeteria bugs. Either one would be a nightmare.

"Don't turn on the overhead light," I whispered. "We don't want anyone to notice a light in here. Besides, it might scare off the roaches."

We both shuddered in the darkness. I just knew that millions of hideous critters would scurry across the floor—across my feet!—to their secret hiding places.

Switching on our flashlights, we tiptoed around the kitchen. Our beams of light reflected off stainless steel pots and pans hanging from the ceiling over a central island counter. The huge refrigerator and sinks gleamed also. White counters everywhere. Shiny surfaces galore.

The kitchen was in pristine condition!

"Do you see any bugs?" I whispered.

"No. Do you?"

"Not yet."

I started opening cabinet doors and shining my light inside. But all I saw were more pots and pans, all types of skillets and cookware, plastic containers, restaurant-size cans of food, and boxes of trash bags.

The drawers revealed flatware, cooking utensils, dish towels, rolling pins, and strange gadgets I didn't recognize at all. The ovens and the stove were spotless.

Not a bug, a cobweb, or a speck of dirt in sight.

What kind of school kitchen was this, anyway?

Soft light from the industrial-size refrigerator brightened the kitchen. I turned around and saw Belinda with her head stuck inside, checking out today's leftovers.

"Any bugs?" I asked hopefully.

"Nope, but the banana pudding tastes great!" She licked her index finger.

"We didn't have banana pudding today."

"Must be for tomorrow."

I wrinkled my nose. "Oh yuck. Your germs are in it now."

"Give me a break," she said, sticking her finger back in the container, "like there aren't millions of germs in here already."

"Uh, Belinda, this kitchen is incredibly clean."

She closed the door to the refrigerator, and in the light of my flashlight I saw the look of disappointment on her face. "I know," she said softly. "Not even slime in the ice machine. My own mother, Mrs. Clean, would be envious."

Sweeping my light around the room again, I said, "There have to be at least a couple of bugs somewhere! How can a school cafeteria look this good?"

I climbed onto the counter island to inspect the hanging pots and pans. They rattled and clanged.

"Shhh!" Belinda whispered. "They'll hear us!"

Finally I silenced them and climbed back

down. "Maybe they just cleaned up really well because of all that bug business at lunch today."

"Maybe," Belinda said. "But I don't think they could get it this clean in that short amount of time."

"So what do we do now?" I asked. "Operation Bug Hunt is a failure."

Without commenting, Belinda walked over to the swinging doors. I thought she was about to leave, but instead she slid her hand down the wall until she found the light switch.

Before I could say no, she'd flicked on the overhead fluorescent lights.

"Why'd you do that?" I asked angrily. "Someone might see the light!"

She frowned, her shoulders sagging. "I was hoping that maybe a roach or even an ant would run and hide from the light."

"No such luck." I leaned against the center island. "Turn off the light, and let's get out of here."

"Yeah. We'll make the late bus in plenty of time." Her voice sounded as sad as I felt. She clicked off the light, and we were plunged into darkness again.

"All that work for nothing," I said.

Discouragement weighed us down. We didn't even bother turning on our flashlights. What was the use? We just walked through the swinging kitchen doors.

Smack dab into the folded arms of Mrs. Matzke.

chapter

11

Detention!

Belinda and I got D-Hall after school the next day. We also got lectures from just about every adult who saw us.

"Just what do you think you're doing?" Mrs. Matzke had asked us, disapproval dripping from her voice.

"I'm so disappointed in you," Mrs. Kopecky had said. She'd sounded tired, and her glasses looked droopy.

"You did *what* in my locker room?" Miss Crowell's eyebrows had tried to reach her hairline.

We didn't have to wait for the late bus. Mrs. Kopecky called our parents to come pick us up, and, by the way, have a chat with her. Well, it wasn't really a chat, more like a sermon on the world's worst sinners. Mrs. Kopecky could take up preaching if she ever got tired of principaling.

The ride home was silent. I kept glancing over at Mom, whose face was red from embarrassment and anger. Not a good combination.

She parked in the driveway, turned to me, and said, "Just you wait until your father comes home."

My life had turned into a bad cliché.

Then I was sent upstairs to my room to think about my actions. I thought about them, okay, and I really didn't think breaking into the cafeteria kitchen was such a big crime. I mean, we didn't steal anything . . . except for Belinda's fingerful of pudding. We didn't vandalize anything. All we wanted was to rid the school of a few insects, and everyone acted as if we were trying to take the royal jewels.

How was I to know that the school exterminated on a regular basis and that the health inspector was rather picky about the state of the cafeteria?

I threw myself across my bed, put on my headphones, and listened to my favorite CD. But even that didn't improve my mood.

I was doomed.

If I had to stay in my room forever, I'd never collect all the bugs I needed. I'd fail science, drop out of school, and become a criminal. And Alexander would probably grow up to be a respected scientist.

Life just wasn't fair!

My door creaked open, and Alexander poked his head in. "Meggie?"

I lifted my headphones off one ear. "What do you want?"

"Did you really sneak into the school kitchen?"

I put my headphones back in place. "None of your business."

He pushed the door open all the way and walked inside my room.

"Get out!" I yelled.

"Are you in trouble now?"

"You little pest! I hate you! It's all your fault. Get out of my room!" I hurled a pillow at him, hitting him in the chest.

His face crumbled. He turned and ran out of my room.

I was mad at Alexander for coming into my room without knocking, for stealing my bugs, for having no respect for my privacy. I was mad at him for causing me to be in this mess. I was mad at my parents for allowing this to happen. For not getting me a lock for my door. At Charlie for teasing me so much. At Belinda for turning on the light and getting us caught.

I was mad at the world!

Maybe part of the blame for my current problem rested on me and my rash ideas. Maybe . . . but just a small part.

Dad came home early. I knew I was really in trouble then.

Reluctantly I dragged myself downstairs and sat on the couch opposite the TV in the family room. Mom sat in the chair facing the fireplace. Dad sat on the other end of the couch from me.

Mom frowned. Dad frowned. I frowned.

We all sat silently with our arms crossed.

Mom broke the silence. "Megan Elaine Hollander, I just don't understand. What on earth were you doing in the school kitchen?"

I didn't say anything, just studied my shoes.

84

Dad ran his fingers through his thinning hair. "Well, what I don't understand is how this all started."

"It's because I need a lock on my door," I mumbled, still staring at my suddenly fascinating sneakers.

"A lock!" Mom's eyes widened. "What does that have to do with vandalizing the school cafeteria?"

"We didn't hurt anything." I refused to look at her, but I narrowed my eyes and clenched my teeth so hard that a muscle in my jaw started twitching.

"Wait a minute," Dad said. "Let's go back. Megan, what do you mean about needing a lock? What does that have to do with this situation?"

I sighed and looked up at him. "I need a lock on my bedroom door. I'm tired of Alexander always going into my room and messing with my stuff." I said it as patiently as possible, without sounding rude . . . hopefully. I was already in plenty of trouble.

Now it was Mom who narrowed her eyes as she stood up. "We've told you we'll get you a lock. You know how busy we've been. I'm trying to get ready for the craft shows, and your father—"

Dad cut her off, waving his hand like a traffic cop. "Calm down, Cindy."

"Calm down? You didn't have to sit in the principal's office like I did." Mom paced the room. "What she and Belinda did was serious!"

"Cindy, let Megan finish. Let's hear what she has to say first."

My mother sat back in her chair, her lips pulled into a thin, tight line. Both of my parents stared at me, waiting.

I took a deep breath. "Well, you see, I have this major science project. And Alexander keeps stealing the bugs I've collected for it, and I have to keep finding more." I bit my lip, trying not to cry. Where was that defiance I'd felt just a moment ago? "And that's why I need a lock. To keep him out."

Mom said nothing, but I could tell she wanted to. Dad just looked puzzled.

"Okay," he said. "You need a lock on your door to keep Alexander from stealing your bugs. But what does that have to do with breaking into the school kitchen?"

I looked down at my shoes again, but my vision was blurry with unshed tears. "We didn't break in. The door was unlocked."

"So why'd you go in there?" I knew he was trying to be patient—and that I wasn't helping.

"We thought we could catch some bugs for our project."

Dad looked at me thoughtfully for a moment. Then his eyebrows unpuckered and the corners of his lips twitched. "You thought the school kitchen was full of insects?"

I nodded.

Suddenly he laughed, a great big booming laugh. It made me stare at him. Seeing him laughing made me want to laugh, too. My lips twitched.

"What an ingenious idea!" He laughed so hard, he had to wipe his eyes.

My mother, however, saw the situation entirely differently. "Young lady," she said, frowning, "what do you mean going where you're not allowed? We've taught you to respect other people's property and to obey the rules. What you did today was inexcusable. That's *not* how we act in this family!"

"But, Mom," I said meekly, "you and Dad don't care when Alexander acts like that."

"Your baby brother does *not* act like—"

"Wait a minute, Cindy. She's right." Dad was no longer laughing, but serious once more. "And

Alexander's not the only one who acts that way. We do, too."

The frown left her face, shock replacing it. "What on earth are you talking about, Jack?"

"We allow Alexander to enter Megan's room whenever he wants. We allow him to play with her things . . . take her bugs. And what do we do about it?" He shrugged. "Nothing."

Mom protested, "But . . . but this is different."

"How?"

I sat there, staring at my parents, amazed at the change of events.

"Well, for one thing, Alexander's just a baby. He doesn't know any better . . . and I guess I thought Megan would have no trouble getting more bugs. . . ." Mom's voice trailed off.

Dad shook his head. "He's not a baby anymore. He's five and in kindergarten. When Megan was that age, we'd already taught her to respect closed doors. She must have felt pretty desperate to do what she did today."

My mother's face changed from shock to puzzlement to realization. She sagged back into her chair like a balloon losing air. "I guess I never thought of it that way before."

Turning to me, Dad said, "Megan, what you did was wrong, but you already know that. I want you to write an apology to everyone involved. That will be your punishment, besides detention tomorrow."

I smiled and wiped the back of my hand across my eyes. I'd have to write about a million letters, but that was better than being sentenced to my room for the rest of my life.

"And," my father continued, "when I get back from my business trip, I'll make sure you have a lock for your door."

Mom jumped in. "I'll talk to Alexander about leaving your bugs alone."

Things were looking up. Maybe I'd pass science after all and not have to lead a life of crime.

And then I remembered what I faced tomorrow. My parents might be understanding, but I wasn't so sure about the teachers at DeMitri Intermediate. I'd heard horror stories.

Detention would be the pits!

chapter 12

Our raid on the kitchen was all over school the next day.

Mrs. Tennyson lectured our science class about doing the project correctly, that it was supposed to be educational.

Lenora Bell stopped me and Belinda in the hall after class. "You've got Mrs. Tennyson upset!"

We ignored her. Lenora was such a teacher's pet that if she found out a teacher liked cats, she'd start meowing.

"My sister will be coming here next year, and you're going to mess things up for her," Lenora announced. "What if Mrs. Tennyson is so upset she decides to do a different project? My sister really wants to collect insects."

I glanced at Belinda, and she raised an eyebrow. Lenora has a sister? Oh no!

"You'd better be on your best behavior," Lenora warned. "I don't want my sister to be disappointed."

"Gee, me neither." I rolled my eyes.

Tamika barged between Lenora and me and gave me and Belinda high fives. "Y'all are braver than I thought! Tackling the cafeteria kitchen like that." She winked. "I'm impressed!"

And that's the way the kids viewed Belinda and me. Either, like Lenora, they were shocked by our behavior. Or, like Tamika, they were impressed. Our fame—or notoriety—spread throughout DeMitri Intermediate. Heroes or villains, either way, we had a reputation now.

That afternoon after school, I trudged down to D-Hall alone. I presented myself to Miss Rosenbloom, who was in charge of Thursday D-Halls. I didn't think she'd view me as a hero.

Belinda, the traitor, got off the hook for the day because she had an orthodontist's appointment that couldn't be changed. Why couldn't I have been born with crooked teeth and need braces?

Miss Rosenbloom assigned me a seat, and I looked around for the ball and chain that I just knew they'd attach to my ankle. She handed me a list of rules, and I read them silently at my temporary desk.

No talking.

No food or drinks.

No bathroom breaks.

No. No. No.

I was glad to see I was allowed to breathe.

Just as I had resigned myself to an afternoon of misery, thinking things couldn't get much worse . . . they did.

Charlie Bettencourt walked through the door.

He showed Miss Rosenbloom his dimpled smile, and she showed him his new seat—next to mine.

Thank goodness for the silence. Charlie wasn't allowed to say a word.

As soon as the rest of the school had left and only the kids staying for tutorials were still around, Miss Rosenbloom frowned at us. "Now I'll give out your work assignments."

Work? I'd never been in serious trouble

before. I didn't have a clue what happened in D-Hall. Only that you didn't want to go there. Ever.

Miss Rosenbloom divided us into crews and handed out trash bags. Unfortunately, Charlie was assigned to my crew. Our job was to pick up trash around the building. Great! Now all the stragglers who hadn't been picked up by their parents would see me.

Dejected, I walked outside, avoiding Charlie, and started scooping up gum wrappers and soda cans near the band hall.

Bend over. Pick up. Stuff in bag. Was that a saxophone playing the scales? Bend over. Pick up. Stuff in bag. A French horn? Bend over. Pick up—

A hand stopped me from automatically stuffing old newspaper into the bag. I looked up. Charlie.

"Did you and Belinda really do it?"

I shook off his hand and finished stuffing in the newspaper. "We aren't supposed to be talking."

"Why'd you do it?"

I tried to walk around him, but he blocked my path. "I needed more bugs," I hissed.

He seemed puzzled. "You really care about this, don't you?"

"Yes."

"But why? You're not a nerd like Lenora."

"Gee, thanks."

He grinned. "So why is this project so important to you? It's just a bunch of stupid bugs."

"Look, I'm not that great in science. I just figured that this project would be an easy way to raise my grade. Boy, was I wrong."

"But breaking into the kitchen?" He laughed. "I'm shocked!"

"Give me a break," I fumed. "You just wish you'd thought of it first."

"No, Lenora wishes she'd thought of it first."

"Go away. We're not even supposed to be talking."

He stepped aside but didn't leave. Instead, he picked up trash beside me. We continued being silent garbage collectors.

Bend over. Pick up. Stuff in bag.

I never realized how much trash there was. It was a windy day, and all sorts of things blew around the campus. Bottle tops. Straws. Broken pencils. Pieces of paper. The lawn around the school never looked bad, but, then again, I'd never really looked at it this close up before. The wind blew trash into the bushes around the school's foundation and into the ditches next to the street.

Bend over. Pick up—

"Whoa!" I said, pushing aside a fast-food cup near a bush. "A stinkbug!"

Charlie jumped away. I picked up the cup and slowly slid it over the branch where the green shield-shaped beetle sat. These things smell nasty if you disturb them, and I sure didn't want it to live up to its name. I broke off the branch and lifted the cup upright. When I peered inside, the stinkbug seemed happy enough—if stink-bugs can be happy. Charlie, however, looked distinctly unhappy.

"Want to see it?" I held the cup near Charlie's face.

He held up his hands to ward me off. "No way."

I looked at him thoughtfully. "I'm right, aren't I?"

Warily he answered, "About what?"

Now I smiled, showing all my teeth. "About you being afraid of bugs."

He laughed, but it didn't sound genuine. "Oh, come off it."

"Why are you afraid?"

"Who says I'm afraid?"

"I do."

"Well, you're wrong." Charlie turned on his heel and started picking up trash again, walking ahead of me. I hurried to catch up with him.

"Why won't you just admit it?" I asked. This time I was the one puzzled.

"Give it up, Megan."

"I guess I could ask Hector about it. Or Joe Davis. Or maybe Peter—"

"Just shut up, Megan," he said angrily. "You don't know what you're talking about."

"So you tell me."

He glared at me. "It's none of your business."

"I wonder what Belinda would say. . . ." I let my voice trail off, hoping this would force him to tell me. I couldn't understand a guy like him being afraid of bugs. It didn't make sense.

Charlie frowned harder but didn't take my bait. He ignored me as he picked up trash. We worked silently again for a long time, side by side.

Bend over. Pick up. Stuff in bag. Bend over. Pick up. Stuff in bag.

Then he turned to me. "Listen, how about a truce?"

"A truce? Are we at war?"

"Well, yeah. I think we are now."

"How would this truce work?"

"I'll stop teasing you, if—" He glanced behind him, then lowered his voice. "If you don't tell anyone about, you know, uh . . ."

"You being afraid of bugs?"

Charlie crossed his arms in front of him and frowned. "I'm not afraid. I just don't like them."

I crossed my arms, too, and frowned just as hard. "You are too afraid."

He stuffed his hands in his pockets. "Look, Megan, don't go around blabbing things to people, okay? I'm not afraid of stupid bugs." His eyes pleaded with mine. "I won't ever tease you again . . . about anything. Okay? Truce?" He held his hand out to me.

"No more bug jokes?"

"No."

"No more bugs in my lunch?"

"No."

"No more announcements about me on the blackboard?"

"No."

I took his hand and we shook. "Okay. Truce."

We went back to picking up litter. We didn't say anything for a long time.

"So, Charlie," I finally said, "do you need help with your science project?"

"Naw."

"You'll fail without it."

"Yeah, well, those are the breaks."

"They don't have to be."

"Just what are you suggesting?" he asked.

"I promised my mother last night I'd take my little brother to the park to get him out of her hair. You can come if you want, and we can look for bugs."

"I don't like bugs."

"You don't have to. Alexander loves them. I won't tell anyone how you feel, and you can have some insects for science."

Once again he turned away from me and silently began to pick up trash. Then he dropped his bag and turned back to face me.

"When are you going?"

"Tomorrow after school. Mom has to finish her ceramic angels for a craft show this weekend."

"What about Belinda?"

"My partner in crime has to do her time in D-Hall tomorrow."

"Okay." Then he went back to filling his bag with trash.

What had I done? I'd just committed myself to an afternoon in the park with the two biggest pests in my life.

chapter 13

I pushed Alexander on the swing at the park. His shaggy brown hair flew everywhere. As soon as Mom's craft show was over, she'd better take him to get a haircut.

"Higher, Meggie! Faster!"

I gave him an extra-hard push, and he shot forward, feet pointing to the sky, laughter floating on the wind.

Last night I'd apologized to Alexander. I didn't really hate him. In fact, I actually liked him when he wasn't stealing my bugs or messing with the things in my room.

Before Dad left for his business trip yesterday, we'd talked some more. He'd said that a lot of

Mom's anger was stress about the upcoming craft shows. I'd noticed Mom had dark circles under her eyes and the paint never seemed to come off her fingers. Well, if taking my brother to the park would help, I was all for it.

"Hey, Meggie?"

"Yeah?"

"Can we go feed the ducks?"

"Yeah."

The swing slowed and my brother jumped off, sending dust clouds and dead leaves swirling. He ran to get his backpack, which we'd stuffed with stale bread, his insect books, butter tubs, and a fishnet.

I could tell Alexander was really enjoying this outing. Why hadn't I ever done anything like this with him before?

We were waiting for Charlie to meet us there after school, before we started our bug collecting. I was a little nervous about having a bug lover and a bug hater together in the same park. An all-out insect war could break out if I didn't handle things carefully. How did I get myself into these situations?

Several ducks swam in the park's little pond. Alexander tossed chunks of bread at them. They greedily quacked and thrashed the water, gobbling up his offering. Then they waddled ashore and surrounded us, wanting more bread. We laughed and gave them what they wanted. But as soon as the bread ran out, so did their attention, and they returned to the pond to swim in lazy circles.

Alexander squatted near the edge of the water where a clump of weeds grew. "Meggie! Look at the bugs!"

I knelt next to him. Floating on the water surface were a whole bunch of bugs that looked like shiny black watermelon seeds. "They're funny-looking, aren't they?"

"What're you looking at?"

I glanced up and saw Charlie. "Bugs, of course. No D-Hall today?"

"Nope. I was on my best behavior."

"Hey, Meggie," Alexander said, interrupting us. "Touch one of the bugs."

"What's it going to do?" I asked suspiciously.

He giggled. "Come on, Meggie, touch one."

Scrunching up my face as well as my courage, I reached down. The little watermelon seeds started milling around rapidly, circling and spinning. I laughed.

"What are those things?" Charlie asked.

I shrugged. "Ask Alexander. He's the expert."

My brother beamed. "They're whirligigs. Beetles."

Charlie looked impressed. "How old are you?"

"Five."

"And you know stuff like this?"

Alexander nodded. "Mom reads to me about all kinds of bugs. I like to look at the pictures." He pulled a book out of his backpack. "This one's my favorite," he said, hugging it.

"Sometimes he sleeps with it," I confided.

Wrinkling his nose, Charlie said, "I'd have nightmares."

"Are you afraid of bugs?" Alexander asked.

Charlie glared at me. But I shook my head and pretended to zip my lips.

"I just don't like them that much, kid, that's all," he said gruffly.

My brother looked thoughtful. "Oh. Because some people are afraid of them. Some of them bugs look kind of scary, you know?"

"Yeah," Charlie said, "and some of them sting."

"You ever been stung?" Alexander asked.

Charlie turned away and stared out at the

ducks swimming on the pond. "Once, but I don't want to talk about it."

Uh-oh. Was this the beginning of the insect war?

"One time," my brother said, "a bee got caught in my hair. When I tried to pull it out, it stung my finger. I think it was a sweat bee, because they sting when you pinch them."

Charlie just kept staring out at the pond.

"Well," I said, trying to change the subject. "Let's catch some of these whirly things." I got out the aquarium fishnet left over from when my father had tried to raise guppies.

"You mean whirligigs," Alexander corrected me.

"Right." We scooped some in the net and put them in the butter tubs. I noticed an unusual odor coming from the beetles. "They kind of smell like apples!"

That made Charlie turn back around and join us again. He actually leaned close to the butter tub and sniffed. "Hey, they do! That's weird."

"Whirligigs are my favorites," Alexander announced.

"I thought ladybugs were," I said.

My brother grinned. "Them too."

We followed Alexander around the pond,

looking for insects to capture. Actually Alexander and I caught the bugs, and Charlie watched. We poked under rocks and leaves and logs. Charlie gave us plenty of working space, but he did admire from a distance the bugs we found.

A bright green ground beetle scurried out from under a stone, and I grabbed it. There seemed to be lots of different kinds of beetles all around the area.

Alexander scooped up a water strider from among the dry leaves near the pond's shore. To me it looked like a slender black roach with really long skinny legs. My brother said it moved across the top of the water as if it were skating. He showed us a picture. I'm not that great at skating. Maybe this bug could give me lessons.

Charlie was more interested in my brother's books than the insects we caught. He started looking at the pictures and reading out loud about some of our bugs.

By the time we had to go home, we'd found plenty of bugs to add to our collections. It had been a good day at the park . . . both for bugs and for boys. Neither Charlie nor Alexander had been a pest. Bug-Lover and Bug-Hater had avoided conflict and actually appeared to like each other. How'd that happen?

We walked home together, my brother chattering on about how water striders were his new favorite bug. Charlie had upheld his part of our truce and hadn't teased me once.

While Alexander was preoccupied with all the bugs we'd caught, I said to Charlie, "I wonder how long I'll have these bugs."

"Talk to him about it," Charlie said. "He's a smart kid."

"I've talked myself blue in the face, trying to convince him to leave my bugs alone. It won't do any good."

Alexander looked up. "What won't do any good?"

Charlie nodded toward my brother. "Go ahead. Talk to him."

The three of us stopped beside the streetlight in front of our house. I sighed. I didn't really believe that my brother would keep our bargain.

"Alexander," I reminded him, "you do know that we're going to have to kill these bugs for our science homework, right?"

His eyes looked watery. "Even the water strider?"

I nodded.

"And the whirligigs?"

"Them too."

"But why do you have to kill them?"

It was getting dark and the streetlight came on, casting faint yellow light around us. "That's how we study them," I told him. "That's how we learn more about them."

"I study them, too," Alexander said, "but I don't have to kill them. I just read about them in my books."

I was getting exasperated. This same old argument kept cropping up, and I didn't really have an answer for it.

Then Charlie spoke up. "How do you think the scientists found out about the bugs?" he asked my brother.

Alexander chewed on his thumbnail. "By watching them? And taking pictures?"

"Yes," Charlie said, "but sometimes they also had to kill them."

Wide-eyed, my brother gasped. "They did? Why?"

"It's hard to see some of the things on insects close up unless you put them under a microscope," he explained. "I don't think most bugs would agree to lie still while you held a magnifying glass over them."

Alexander frowned as he thought about what Charlie had said. "I don't like it that people gotta kill them to study them."

Holding up one of my brother's books, Charlie said, "There's all kinds of great information in here. Water striders have these hairlike things on their feet that push the water down and kind of look like boots or skates. Now, how do you suppose the writer of this book figured that out?"

My brother shrugged.

"He had to study it up close under a microscope, and you know what that means."

"That he had to kill it?" Alexander's eyes widened. "You mean that the pictures in my book are all of *dead* bugs?"

"No, no, not all of them." Charlie flipped the book open to the water strider page. As he did, a moth flitted by his face, searching for the streetlight.

Charlie yelped, threw the book up in the air, and jumped away. The moth fluttered off to find a more peaceful light source.

I have to admit this surprised me. I mean, all afternoon Charlie had kept his distance from the insects, but he'd never reacted this way. How could a harmless little moth upset him and not some of the nastier bugs like the water strider?

Charlie looked embarrassed, his face stained a deep red. He turned away from us and, without saying a word, started to walk home.

Alexander picked up the tossed book, then ran up to him. "Charlie? You can use my bugs. It's okay."

Charlie stopped walking and turned to him. "What?"

"It's okay if you want to kill my bugs. I understand now."

"You mean about the science project?"

My brother shrugged and said softly, "I guess it's a way to learn about bugs." He held out the book. "And you can borrow my book, too."

"What made you change your mind?"

"Because you don't like bugs, and I want you to like them."

Charlie smiled as he took the book. "You're quite a guy. I've never met anyone like you before."

My brother solemnly accepted the compliment. "So why are you afraid of bugs?" he asked innocently.

"Alexander!" I yelled.

But I was too late. One look at Charlie's face and I knew. The insect war had just begun.

chapter
14

Charlie thrust the book back into Alexander's hands. "I told you I just don't like them. That's all."

"But, Charlie," my brother said, trying to give back the book, "I watched you in the park. And I saw you with that moth."

Taking the book, Charlie slammed it on the ground. "Leave me alone! Don't bug me about it anymore!" He started to stomp away.

I'd never seen him this upset before. Charlie, the joker, the teaser, who always had a smile for everything. But not now.

I caught up to him.

"Are you okay? Why are you acting so weird?" I asked.

"Who's acting weird?" He spun around. "Not me. You're making something out of nothing."

"Come on, Charlie," I coaxed. "I know you have a major problem with bugs. Tell me what happened to make you this way."

"Why? So you can blab it to everyone at school?"

"I wouldn't do that. We have a truce, remember?"

"What happened, Charlie?" Alexander asked. He'd picked up his cherished book and clutched it in front of him. "Did you get stung like me? Is that why you don't like flying bugs?"

Judging by Charlie's expression, I could tell Alexander had hit pretty close to home.

The anger left Charlie like water going down a drain. He sat down on the grass with his legs bent in front of him and his elbows crossed on his knees, pillowing his forehead. I couldn't see his face.

"How'd you know?" His voice sounded muffled.

My brother sat down on one side of Charlie. I sat on the other.

"I guessed," Alexander admitted. "Because you sure don't like moths when they fly at you. Was it a bee?"

Charlie was silent for a long time. I shifted uneasily on the grass. Maybe he really wasn't ready yet to talk about it.

"Yellow jackets," he said finally, still not looking up, "when I was about your age."

"One stung you?" I asked.

"Not just one." Charlie raised his head and looked at me. "I was playing hide-and-seek with some neighborhood kids. And I hid in the bushes by my house." His voice was strangely flat as he talked, but I could see fear in his eyes.

"Uh-oh. Yellow jackets and hornets like to build nests in bushes," Alexander said.

"Let him talk," I told my brother. "Go on, Charlie."

He looked at Alexander and nodded. "You're right. There was a big nest right next to the bush where I was hiding. As soon as I saw it, I knew I was in trouble."

"Yeah," Alexander said, "yellow jackets are mean! They'll chase you for no reason."

Charlie nodded again. "I didn't even touch their nest, but that didn't matter. They swarmed me. I couldn't get away. Everywhere I looked, everywhere I ran—there was no escape." There was a catch in his voice as he continued. "They stung me. And stung me. And stung me. It was like I was on fire, it hurt so bad. I screamed and tried to fight them off, but it was no use. By the time my brother found me, I was covered with welts. My face was so swollen, he almost didn't recognize me."

Horror clawed at my stomach. No wonder he was afraid of insects. I would be, too, if that had happened to me! I couldn't help shuddering.

"How horrible," I whispered.

"What happened next?" Alexander asked.

Charlie's voice was soft as he answered. "My parents had to take me to the hospital. I was pretty sick for a while." He paused. "So now you know my deep, dark secret."

"But I don't understand," Alexander said. "How come you're afraid of bugs?"

Charlie sighed. "I just told you."

My brother shook his head. "No. I know why you hate yellow jackets. But why all bugs?"

Shrugging, Charlie said, "All I know is that I still have nightmares sometimes about bugs of all kinds. They're coming at me, flying or crawling, and then they're all over me, biting and stinging."

"Boy, that would make me wake up screaming in the middle of the night," I said.

"Sometimes I do."

I couldn't help looking at Charlie differently. Here was a kid I thought nothing bothered. I was totally wrong. It made me wonder what other dimensions there were to Charlie.

Alexander handed his book back to Charlie. "You really need this book. Bugs aren't scary when you get to know them."

Charlie smiled, showing his dimples, and accepted the book once more. "Maybe you're right. Maybe they won't be so scary."

"And," I added, "you might even grow to like them as much as Alexander does."

"I seriously doubt it." Then he tousled my brother's tangled mop of hair. "You know, I'm going to call you Bug Man. You're incredible. Who would have thought that I'd be reading about bugs, of all things, so I could get to know them!"

Mom stood on the front porch. "Time to come in, Megan and Alexander!"

"I'll be there in a few minutes," I yelled.

Alexander, however, jumped up and grabbed

his backpack. "I gotta show Mom all the little buggies. Bye, Charlie."

He saluted my brother. "See you later, Bug Man."

After Alexander had run inside, I asked, "Does Hector know?"

Charlie shook his head. "I'd never live it down if he did."

"But the other night, you know . . . how you acted with the roach and the moth. Didn't Hector notice at all?"

"Nope. I distracted him by teasing you so much," he explained. "Whenever Hector thought of bugs, he thought of you, not me."

I was silent for a moment, then said softly, "I really hated the teasing."

"I know, and I'm sorry," he said, sounding sincere. "I shouldn't have done that."

"You can be really nice sometimes," I said, "and other times, well—I don't understand that."

He sighed and looked away. "Before we moved here, I used to get teased a lot. About being afraid of bugs and all. After I came out of the hospital, I'd go crazy around bugs. Everyone called me a sissy."

"Society for the Insect–Catching Impaired," I said softly and smiled. "SICI. It is kind of funny."

"Yeah, except when everybody's laughing at you. I'm really sorry about that. I overdid the teasing, didn't I?"

I nodded. "So you move here and end up teasing everyone around you. If you used to get teased, then you should know how bad it feels."

He seemed to be studying the streetlight and all the insects buzzing around it. "My dad's a football coach at the high school, and he always says that the best defense is a good offense. So when we moved here, I took the offensive."

"Well, you certainly have been offensive."

He gave me a fleeting glimpse of dimple. "Yeah, I guess I have."

"Why are you telling me all this?"

Plucking a blade of grass, he said, "I don't know. I guess I never cared before who I teased. But when I teased you, it felt different." The grass twirled between his fingers.

"Different?"

"Yeah, you know, because I like you and all."

He ducked his head, not meeting my eyes. The blade of grass stopped its dance.

Belinda was right!

Charlie, the boy I'd spent all this time being mad at, *liked* me? Charlie, the boy who wasn't what he seemed to be, liked *me?*

Charlie Bettencourt, of all people!

"So," he said, finally raising his head, "do you like me?"

Now what was I supposed to say?

chapter 15

As I thought about how to answer his question, his face changed. At first hope filled his eyes, making them bright blue, his eyebrows raised in expectation. Dimples and white teeth flashed. But as I continued to be silent, his eyes clouded and his eyebrows lowered. His dimples disappeared. Finally his eyes darkened to a stormy blue, his eyebrows furrowed close to his nose, and his mouth pulled down in a tight line.

He turned away from me, the blade of grass dangling from his fingers. "That's okay. You don't have to like me."

"Hey," I said. "I was just trying to figure out

what you meant. Do you mean 'like' as in girl-friend or 'like' as in friend?"

"Does it matter?" His voice sounded sullen as he dropped the blade of grass.

"Yeah, it does. Because I used to not like you at all." I heard him sigh, but I continued. "But now, I don't know. I mean, I've discovered that you're different from what I thought. I had a lot of fun with you and Alexander today at the park."

He gave me a weak smile, no dimples. "Some fun. I wasn't much help collecting bugs."

I laughed. "You were *no* help with the insects. But you have no idea what a great help you were with Alexander! I think you finally convinced him to leave my bugs alone. For that you have my eternal thanks."

He grinned, full dimples. "It was nothing. All I had to do was reveal my deepest, darkest secret to a five-year-old insect scientist."

"And you also have my friendship."

"As in 'just a friend'?"

I nodded.

"You know, I have an older brother in tenth grade who warned me that when a girl says she just wants to be friends, the relationship is over."

I shook my head. "Maybe in high school. But at DeMitri Intermediate it means our friendship is just beginning."

"I like that," he said, standing up. "Well, I've got to go home."

"What about your bugs? Aren't you going to take them?"

He cradled Alexander's book in his arms. "I don't think I'm quite ready for that yet. Can you keep them for me?"

"Sure." We waved good-bye.

Boy, did I have a lot to tell Belinda! Of course, I wasn't about to tell Charlie's secret. I'd promised. But the rest of the stuff—well, Belinda would never forgive me if I didn't.

On the phone she said, "I just knew it! I could tell he liked you a lot." She giggled. "And you thought he was acting weird because he was afraid of bugs."

"Silly me."

"So now he's your boyfriend?"

"No, just a friend."

"Hmmm . . . Charlie Bettencourt as your friend. That'll be interesting."

The next day Alexander and I went back to the park. I guess I could have looked at our park trips as punishment, but I'd had way too much fun yesterday to think that. I chased my brother through piles of dry brown leaves, scattering them as we ran. Then I tackled him and rolled with him through the piles. He squealed and I shrieked, and then we plucked leaves and twigs from our hair.

Charlie showed up as we were chasing squirrels up a tree. "I thought we had to catch bugs, not squirrels," he said, grinning.

"We were just feeling a little nutty," I said.

"Nutty!" Alexander laughed as if it were the best joke ever told.

Charlie, however, just shook his head. "I'm the nutty one for coming back out here."

Alexander took Charlie's hand. "Don't worry," he said, "I know all about bugs—the good ones and the bad ones."

"That you do, Bug Man," he said, "and I trust you."

"Oh, look at the ladybugs." I pointed to some vines where a whole bunch of ladybugs crawled. "I already have one, but aren't they pretty?"

Charlie looked doubtful. "I guess, if bugs can be pretty."

Alexander ran over and examined them closely. "Ladybugs only eat bad bugs, like aphids." He looked up at Charlie. "Did you know that some ladybugs are really boy bugs?"

"So why don't we call them gentlemen bugs?" Charlie asked.

My brother shrugged.

"What? There's something about bugs you don't know?" Charlie pretended to be shocked.

Alexander giggled. "I'm still learning."

My brother was amazing. He already knew more than most people about bugs. So if he was still learning, then *watch out, world!* When he grew up, he'd be the most famous insect scientist in all of history.

We started our bug hunt with Alexander leading the way around the park. He, of course, knew the best places to find insects.

Belinda and Hector found us trying to catch a dragonfly. Alexander had his net and was trying to sneak up on it.

"Oh, man," Hector said. "I never could catch one of those."

"So how many bugs do you have?" I asked.

Hector thumped his chest. "All I need. My bugs are dead, pinned, and labeled. And I have time to spare."

"How about helping us catch this dragonfly?" Charlie suggested.

Hector stepped back. "Hey, I thought you weren't catching any bugs."

"I'm not," Charlie said a little defensively. "Megan needs it."

"You know me," I said, "the girl who's begging for bugs."

Hector laughed, but Belinda smiled knowingly. She whispered to me, "You don't mind his teasing now that he's your boyfriend."

I whispered back, "He's just a friend."

But Belinda ran off, laughing, to chase a horsefly.

Late in the afternoon, we trooped back to my house, tired and happy. We had more bugs to add to our collections, including the dragonfly, which Alexander had finally caught. He'd worked hard to catch it, so I wasn't positive he'd actually give it to me.

I was right. He didn't. He gave it to Charlie instead.

Boys and bugs. Who could figure them out?

The next day Belinda came over with Charlie and Hector. "We want another tour of the insect graveyard," Hector explained. "And I'll pay with bugs. I know you need them."

"Okay," I said, "but I thought you liked it better at night with flashlights."

Charlie grinned, his dimples flashing. "Yeah, but this time we want Alexander to be our tour guide."

So I tagged along as my little brother led the way to Jerome's backyard. Jerome met us back there and the two of them pointed out the sights.

"A mosquito is buried there," Jerome said. "I named him Henry."

"Tamika would be pleased," I said. "She names her bugs, too."

"Did you know that female mosquitoes are the ones that bite?" Charlie asked.

Hector laughed. "So that could be Henrietta, not Henry, buried there."

"The horsefly that Belinda caught is a girl, too," Alexander said. "I know, because it bit me and only the girl horseflies bite."

"So what's buried over there?" Belinda asked.

"A moth," said my brother.

"Sammy," said Jerome.

"Do you know how to tell the difference between a moth and a butterfly?" Charlie asked. "Moths have thicker bodies and their color is duller."

"And they fly at night," Alexander added. "Butterflies fly in the daytime."

Hector shook his head. "We've got two walking, talking insect encyclopedias."

Although Charlie hadn't actually caught any bugs yet, he'd definitely developed an interest in them. I'd created a monster! With Alexander's help, of course.

And my brother had become very helpful. He showed me and Charlie where to find information on our insects. He'd taken a special interest in our project and hadn't stolen any bugs out of my room. Alexander was as proud of our work as we were.

"Thanks," I told him several days later.

"For what, Meggie?"

"For not going in my room without permission."

He grinned. "I don't have to bury the bugs anymore. They're for you and Charlie, so you'll like bugs as much as me."

I doubted that would ever happen. "You've been a big help," I said sincerely.

His smile stretched across his face. "I'm a good teacher for Charlie, aren't I?"

"The best."

"And someday he'll like bugs, won't he?"

"Well, maybe," I said. "Someday."

I was just glad that Charlie had stopped teasing me at school. Instead, everyone had started teasing Charlie about liking me.

"Hey, Charlie," Joe Davis said on the bus, "where's your girlfriend? Aren't you going to kiss her?"

"Yeah," Oscar called, "kiss her!"

Peter started making lip-smacking noises, as if he were kissing the air.

"My *good* friend Megan is sitting up front," Charlie said, flashing his dimples. He then blew kisses all around the bus.

"Oh, man, don't get that kissy stuff on me," Hector complained.

Once again it seemed as if nothing bothered Charlie.

Our science project was due Friday. Thursday night, I pinned the insects and labeled them. Charlie and I each had only twenty-four different kinds. This late in the season it was getting harder and harder to find a good variety.

"Don't worry about it," Charlie said, handing me a pin. "We won't fail with twenty-four. I'll take a B over an F any day."

"But we're so close!" I rolled the pin between my fingers. Mrs. Tennyson had given each student a package of these special scientific insect pins. Very recently I hadn't believed I'd use *any* of them. Now, thanks to Alexander no longer burying my bugs, I only needed one more.

One crummy bug.

Alexander walked into the living room where we were assembling our project. He had his butterfly puppet on both hands, making it swoop here and there. Each hand controlled a wing, and he made the butterfly wave to us.

"Hey, Bug Man!" Charlie greeted him.

"Hi, Charlie. Did you read about the little fireflies?"

"Yeah. Wish we had some around here. Megan and I both need one more bug."

"Meggie, maybe Mom could drive us out to the country," he suggested. "We could find them there."

"Too late. I've pinned my last bug." I dusted off my hands. "Twenty-four will have to do."

Alexander pointed to Charlie with a butterfly wing. "Did ya know that he likes bugs now?"

"Well," Charlie said, looking at me, "it depends on how you define 'like.' "

I poked him. "Are you *friends* with bugs now?"

"Let's just say that I've made my peace with a few insects." He laughed. "We're developing a friendship."

I closed the lids to the two pizza boxes that contained our corkboards of insects. Mrs. Tennyson had suggested these as a good way to transport our projects. Her words, not mine. Anyway, Charlie had painted and decorated them, since I had to do all the handling of the actual insects. He still wouldn't touch a bug.

"Thanks, guys," I said to my two former pests. "I couldn't have done it without you."

The next morning I sat at the breakfast table,

pleased with myself. The project was completed, or as close as it ever would be, and both Charlie and Alexander had kept their promises.

Life was good.

I walked upstairs to get my project. My door was open. And I had definitely closed it before I went down for breakfast.

Only one person would have gone into my room.

Alexander!

chapter 16

That little brat broke his promise!

Storming into my room, I was ready to wring his neck. Maybe I'd even pin *him* to my corkboard as an example of a major pest!

My pizza box had been moved a bit on my desk, and the lid wasn't closed correctly. Holding my breath, I carefully raised the lid.

All my bugs were in place. Just as I had left them.

With one exception.

Alexander had placed one of his toy bugs in the space for the missing insect and labeled it in his crude print. It was a plastic praying mantis, and Mom had had to special order it for Christmas last year.

Taking the praying mantis with me, I ran to Alexander's room. Without giving him a chance to figure out what I was going to do, I swooped him up in a big hug and swung him around the room. Then I gave him a sloppy kiss, which he promptly wiped off.

"Thank you for the thought," I said, handing him back his toy bug, "but my teacher only wants the real thing."

"I just want you to make an A, Meggie."

"I know, and I thank you. You're the best brother a girl could have."

He beamed as he clutched his praying mantis.

I had to hurry to catch my bus. Belinda was waiting eagerly for me.

As I slid onto the bench seat, she whispered, "Charlie's beside himself. He has a special present for you!" She giggled as she balanced her pizza box on her lap. "This is so exciting."

I frowned. A present? I guess I'd have to have a talk with him about "friends" again.

I glanced behind me at Charlie, two rows

back. He was grinning like that Cheshire cat in *Alice in Wonderland*. What was he up to now?

"This is for you," he yelled above all the chatter and noise. Then he passed forward a small box wrapped in tissue paper with a note attached.

Hector and the other boys began making kissing, smacking noises. Instead of being embarrassed, Charlie stood up and bowed. That was Charlie. Nothing bothered him . . . except for a few things that only I knew about.

I laughed and opened the card.

It said: "This is so Megan won't be begging anymore."

Now I frowned. What was going on here? I thought he'd stopped all his teasing. Turning around, I glared at him.

"Open it," he yelled, and made tearing motions with his hands.

Hector led the boys in a chorus of "Open it! Open it! Open it!" They sounded like bullfrogs in the evening around the park pond.

I sighed. Boys were so unpredictable.

"Would you hurry up and open it?" Tamika said.

Belinda nudged me. "If you don't, I will."

With the entire school bus watching, I tore off the tissue paper and opened the lid. Inside, on a bed of cotton, was a dead wasp.

Another note was taped to the inside of the lid: "I didn't kill it. I found it this morning on my porch, already dead. But I did pick it up, and that's a start. From your friend, Charlie 'Bugs Don't Bug Me' Bettencourt."

I looked back at him and gave him a thumbs-up salute. He flashed me his famous dimpled smile and returned the salute.

"What kind of present is that?" Belinda asked.

"The best," I said.

And it really was.